Charlie Joe Jackson's Guide to Kissing Girls

Tommy Greenwald

Charlie Joe Jackson's Guide to

Planet Girl

Illustrations by J. P. Coovert

SQUARE
FISH

Roaring Brook Press ✳ New York

I think I love you—so what am I so afraid of?
—The Partridge Family, "I Think I Love You"

To my friends and colleagues
at Spotco Advertising and in the Broadway Community.
As day jobs go, it's the best there is.

SQUARE
FISH

An imprint of Macmillan Publishing Group, LLC
175 Fifth Avenue, New York, NY 10010
mackids.com

Our books may be purchased in bulk for promotional, educational, or business use. Please contact your
local bookseller or the Macmillan Corporate and Premium Sales Department at (800) 221-7945 ext.
5442 or by e-mail at MacmillanSpecialMarkets@macmillan.com.

Library of Congress Cataloging-in-Publication Data

Greenwald, Tom.
    Charlie Joe Jackson's guide to girls / Tommy Greenwald ; illustrated by J. P. Coovert.
    pages cm. — ([Charlie Joe Jackson series ; 5])
    Summary: "Everyone has a girlfriend except Charlie Joe! But he won't be left in the dust. Look out for
make-ups, break-ups, and hilarious romance tips as Charlie Joe figures out this crazy little thing called
love"—Provided by publisher.
    ISBN 978-1-250-11503-4 (paperback)   ISBN 978-1-59643-843-9 (ebook)   [1. Middle schools—
Fiction.   2. Schools—Fiction.   3. Dating (Social customs)—Fiction.   4. Interpersonal relations—
Fiction.   5. Humorous stories.]   I. Coovert, J. P., illustrator.   II. Title.
    PZ7.G8523Cgg 2015
    [Fic]—dc23

                                                                                    2014047688

Originally published in the United States by Roaring Brook Press
First Square Fish edition, 2017
Book designed by Andrew Arnold
Square Fish logo designed by Filomena Tuosto

10 9 8 7 6 5 4 3 2 1

AR: 4.4

INTRODUCTION

It's time to get serious.

It's time to talk about girls.

All those earlier books? About not reading, and ice cream sandwiches, and musicals about paper towels, and going on strike at Camp Rituhbukkee, and jumping over cows to make money?

That was just a warm-up.

Things are about to get REAL, people.

Because when it comes right down to it, girls are the most important thing in the world. And the ability to deal with girls like a regular person, without breaking out in a cold sweat and stammering like a lunatic, is quite possibly the key to a happy and successful life.

And who knows? You might even wind up with a real, live, actual girlfriend as a result. Or a friend who's a girl, at least.

(As for you girls out there: You can take everything I say and just turn it around, even though for some reason it seems like it's easier for girls to talk to guys than it is for guys to talk to girls. Yet another way in which you're more advanced humans than we are.)

So sit back, relax, and enjoy the story of how I explored the fascinating planet of these mysterious creatures.

If you carefully study everything I did, you'll be fine.

As long as you do the opposite.

Part One
THE LOVE DOCTOR

I have an announcement to make: The middle school years are the best years of your life.

Oh sure, I know what some people say. They say, "Just get through middle school, and everything will get better after that."

Well, if you ask me, those people are crazy.

Listen, I get that it's not for everyone, but I happen to LOVE middle school. It's really fun. The homework is a little hard, but not ridiculously hard. The books you have to read are a little too long—five pages is too long, if you ask me—but not ridiculously long. You don't have all the crazy pressures of high school, like my older sister, Megan, does. And there's still recess! I mean, come on, people! Life is good!

Except for one problem.

I don't have a girlfriend.

Here's the thing: When kids are just starting middle school, guys and girls still haven't really figured each other out yet. At *all*. They circle each other, like two dogs who have just been put in the same cage together for the first time. They think they *should* be friends, they *want* to be friends, but they just don't know *how* to go about it yet.

But then, as middle school goes on, it starts to happen. The huge ocean between girls and guys becomes a river.

Then, a stream.

Then, a puddle.

And finally, the next thing you know, Timmy McGibney is yelling in my ear, "I have a girlfriend!"

Which is exactly what happened at lunch one day.

I looked up from my lukewarm meatball hero and snorted in Timmy's general direction. "Right." Timmy was not exactly a chick magnet. There was that one two-week period where he dated the former girl of my dreams, Hannah Spivero, which should have improved his overall status with the ladies. But sadly, he'd come up empty ever since.

"I'm serious, I do," he said, with a mouthful of ice cream sandwich on full display. "Erica Pope said yes."

"Erica Pope?" I rolled my eyes. Erica was *wwwayy* out of Timmy's league.

"Yup. Apparently she has a thing for lacrosse players." Timmy was my oldest, closest, and most annoying friend, but there was one thing that no one could argue about: He was by far the best lacrosse player in our grade.

"Well, I'll believe it when I see it," I said.

About eight seconds later, I saw it.

Erica came up to Timmy, gave him a big hug, then whispered, "See you after Spanish" in his ear, and ran off.

Timmy looked at me with a way-too-big smile. "Like I was saying."

I shook my head and stared into my chocolate milk. Times were definitely changing. Oh sure, Jake Katz was still going out with Hannah, and Phil Manning and Celia Barbarossa were already acting like an old married couple, but for the past year, they'd been pretty much the only real couples in the grade.

Oh, wait. I forgot about Katie and Nareem.

You know who I'm talking about, right? Katie Friedman and Nareem Ramdal were a pretty hot-and-heavy couple too there, for a while. But they broke up a few months ago. I was sad for them, but a part of me wasn't sad, because Katie's been my unofficial best friend for

7

practically forever, and I guess I was a little jealous that she had a boyfriend. Which felt very weird at the time.

So anyway, Timmy chattered on happily about Erica for another minute. I wasn't really paying attention, though, until I heard two words I'd never heard in the same sentence before: *Pete* and *dating*.

I looked up. "What did you just say?"

"Pete's dating her best friend, and they're coming to the movies with us on Saturday night."

"Pete's dating Mareli?" I was shocked. Mareli was the girl who had moved from Puerto Rico around a year ago. She was a really sharp dresser. According to Eliza Collins, she had the most amazing earring collection of anyone in the school—and she seemed way too sophisticated for Pete Milano. Actually, now that I think about it, a warthog is too sophisticated for Pete Milano.

"Mareli likes Pete," Timmy confirmed. "She thinks he's really funny. And she thinks it's really cool that his family keeps chickens." It was true. Pete's family had been raising chickens ever since I'd known him. According to him, the eggs were delicious. "And they make great pets," he'd say. "Although they don't play fetch or anything."

But back to the matter at hand. "So they're going out?" I asked Timmy.

"Yup," he said. "He asked her out today."

Pete always had a lot of guts—I'll give him that.

"So do you want to come?" Timmy added.

I blinked. "Huh? Come where?"

"To the movies. A lot of us are going."

"Like who?"

Timmy smiled, as if he knew what he was about to say would annoy me, which it did. "Oh, Hannah and Jake, Phil and Celia, Pete and Mareli, Erica and me, and I think Katie and Nareem even though they're not going out anymore, and I think that new kid Emory is going to ask Eliza."

"Emory? No way." Things were getting weirder and weirder. Eliza Collins was the golden girl of Eastport Middle School, and no one had ever had the nerve to ask her out. Now some new kid was going to do it?

"Yes *way*. Emory is from California," Timmy added, as if that explained everything.

I took a swig of chocolate milk and sighed deeply. Then I considered my options: go to the movies and watch a lot of couples hug and possibly even kiss, or sit at home and listen to my parents talk to my sister, Megan, about which colleges she should apply to.

Hey, wait a second.

Remember that whole "middle school years are the best years of your life" thing?

I take it all back.

When it came right down to it, the decision was pretty easy. I went to the movies.

It was some goofy movie about a guy who can't tell his girlfriend he loves her, so then he and his girlfriend get in a fight, and when he goes to bed she puts a spell on him. When he wakes up, he discovers that he cries every time he hears the word *love*, and he gets really embarrassed at work. Eventually he understands that he's become a better person, and then he wakes up and realizes it was all a dream, and he's relieved, but secretly he's worried because he thinks he might go back to the unfeeling person he was before.

Anyway, it had a few laughs before it got all annoyingly lesson-y and moral-y at the end. Why do movies do that all the time?

Afterward, we all went down to Jookie's for a milkshake and snacks.

We sat in two booths: the couples in one and the noncouples in the other.

Which meant that Jake, Hannah, Phil, Celia, Timmy, Erica, Pete, Mareli, Emory, and Eliza were all at one table (apparently Emory and Eliza had officially decided to

become a couple at some point during the first twenty minutes of the movie).

And Katie, Nareem, and I were at the other table.

"It's great to see that you guys can be friends and everything after breaking up," I said. "It's really cool."

Nareem stared at his soda. "It's actually quite difficult, if you want to know the truth."

"Oh," I said.

That ended the conversation for a while. I sat there, eating my cheeseburger and trying to balance a spoon on the end of my nose. It took me a few tries, but I did it.

"Look," I said, showing off my accomplishment.

"Yippee," Katie said, without the slightest enthusiasm.

"Well done," said Nareem.

We took a few more bites of our food.

"Hey, Rituhbukkee Reunion Weekend is coming up," Katie said, trying to think of something that would cheer us all up. Camp Rituhbukkee—pronounced *Read-a-bookie*, by the way—was the school-like summer camp the three of us all went to last year. I totally hated it, for about four days. Then I kind of tolerated it, for about three more days. Then for about a week, I thought it was decent. By the time I left, I completely didn't want to leave.

The reunion was happening in New York City in a couple of weeks, and it was going to be awesome.

"Hey, yeah!" I said, glad to have something fun to look forward to.

Katie smiled. "Do you think Jared Bumpers will be there?" Nareem and I laughed. Jared was the kid who got kicked out of camp on the last day because he was a cheater.

"I doubt it," I said.

"It would certainly be an ironic turn of events," Nareem added, showing off his unfair vocabulary, as usual.

I thought about camp for a minute. One of the reasons it was so fun is that everyone else who went there was . . . let me see, how can I put this without sounding insulting . . . supernerdy. I was the total cool kid. In fact, Camp Rituhbukkee was where I first gave someone girl advice. He was this tall dorky kid named George Feedleman, who ended up becoming one of my closest friends. Yeah. They all thought I was such a stud. A total ladies' man.

Boy, were they wrong.

"You know something?" I said. "This stinks."

Nareem stopped midbite, which isn't easy when you're

eating fried cheese sticks. Once you get going on those things, it's almost impossible to slow down.

"What stinks?" he asked.

I let out a big sigh. "Well, maybe *stinks* is too strong a word, but it's weird. All of a sudden I'm like the only one I know without a girlfriend. I feel like such a loser."

Katie and Nareem looked at each other, and I suddenly realized that since they didn't have boyfriends or girlfriends, either, I'd just kind of called them losers, too.

"Sorry, you guys," I said. "I didn't mean you. At least . . . well . . . I guess what I meant was, I've *never* had a girlfriend."

And there it was. I said it—the sad truth. *I've never had a girlfriend.* Technically, I'd almost had a girlfriend once. Her name was Zoe Alvarez, and we definitely liked each other, but then she moved away, and a few embarrassing misunderstandings later, we'd decided to just be friends. And Eliza Collins, the generally acknowledged prettiest girl in the grade, had always liked me, but for some crazy reason, I didn't like her back. Anyway, the next thing I knew, it was getting late in my middle school career, and I'd never been able to say the four sweetest words in the English language.

Yeah, we're going out.

"Well, I'm sure your luck will change soon," Nareem said, in his typical nicest-person-on-the-planet way. "You're funny and smart, and any girl would be lucky to go out with you."

"Stop being so sweet, Nareem," Katie said. "It's possible Charlie Joe will go through his entire life without knowing the love of a decent woman."

"Ha-ha," I said.

"Ha-ha yourself," Katie said.

Then my chocolate milkshake came. One thing I learned a long time ago: If you're ever feeling really sorry for yourself, order a chocolate milkshake.

I took a long sip, and suddenly things didn't seem so bad.

"Maybe you need to do a little research," Katie suggested.

"What do you mean by that?"

Nareem answered before Katie could. "She means if you want to figure out the mercurial ways of the fairer sex, you may wish to seek counsel from an expert in the field."

Huh?

"Plain English, Nareem," I begged. "Just this once."

Katie laughed. "What we both mean," she said, "is read a book."

I nearly spit milkshake through my nose. "Ha!" But then I looked over at the couples' table, where Pete and Timmy had their arms around their girlfriends. They'd never looked happier in their lives. *Timmy! Pete! Girlfriends!*

They saw me and waved. Timmy whispered something to Pete, and they both snickered. I was sure it was about my miserable, girlfriendless life.

I turned back to Katie and Nareem and sighed.

"How long does this book have to be?"

"**Charlie Joe Jackson,** as I live and breathe!" said Mrs. Reedy, the librarian. "Be still my heart!"

I shrugged my shoulders. "What's the big deal? You act like you've never seen a student before."

"I've seen plenty of students," she said. "But *this* student! My oh my oh my!"

I eye-rolled. "Oh, stop being all dramatic."

The funny thing is, even though Mrs. Reedy and I were almost never in the same room together—mainly because her room happened to be the library, and my room happened to be any room *besides* the library—we got along really well. She and Ms. Ferrell, my guidance counselor, were two of my favorite adults at school.

"In any event," Mrs. Reedy said, "to what do I owe the honor of your special visit?"

I looked around to make sure no one else was listening. The coast was clear. "Well, to be honest," I whispered, "I'm looking for a book."

"A book!" Mrs. Reedy exclaimed in exaggerated shock. Then she saw the look on my face—which was probably half nervousness, half embarrassment—and decided to stop being silly. "What about?" she asked.

"It's hard to say," I admitted. "I guess . . . well . . . do you have any books about how to get girls to like you and want to go out with you?"

Mrs. Reedy looked skeptical. "Are you serious? I've always considered you the man with the silver tongue."

I wasn't sure what that meant, but I was pretty sure it was a compliment.

"Thanks, I guess. But . . . the thing is, I've never had a girlfriend, and I'm thinking maybe I'm doing something wrong or something."

"You're not 'doing something wrong or something,'" Mrs. Reedy said, her warm eyes crinkling into a smile. "You're in middle school. These things take time."

"I don't *have* time," I said. "All my friends have girlfriends all of a sudden, and I'm feeling left out."

"Aha," Mrs. Reedy said quietly. "Do you have a lucky lady in mind?"

"Nope, no one in particular," I said, wanting to end this part of the conversation as quickly as possible.

"I see."

"Also," I added, "the book has to say all the important stuff on the inside flap, the back cover, and the first and last chapters, since those are the only parts I'll be reading."

"Ah, that's the Charlie Joe I know and love," Mrs. Reedy said. Then she clapped her hands together. "Wait a second! I have an idea . . ." She started searching through the stacks.

"There is a book . . . I know it's around here somewhere . . ."
Finally she lit up in a bright smile. "Ah! Here it is!" Mrs.
Reedy picked up a skinny book (just the way I like 'em) and
handed it to me. The back cover was a picture of a boy and
girl sitting at a picnic table and laughing. They were
dressed like they were from a different planet.

"How old is this book?" I asked Mrs. Reedy.

"Older than you," she said. "Possibly even older than
me. But good advice never goes out of style."

I flipped the book over and read the title.

A Communication Guide for Boys and Girls.

I was immediately insulted.

"Wait a second. Are you saying I can't communicate with girls?"

Mrs. Reedy laughed. "Of course I'm not saying that, Charlie Joe," she said. "But it sounds like perhaps you're having a little trouble being yourself around girls. Or at least, you're *worried* that you're not being yourself. That's usually the tricky part. Too much worrying, and not enough relaxing."

I thought about what she said. Maybe she was right. I had a history of trying to be the funniest, wackiest kid all the time. Maybe I tried a little too hard. Maybe Erica liked Timmy because he was just a typical kid. And Pete didn't *try* to be obnoxious all the time—he just *was* obnoxious all the time. I guess Mareli liked that.

I sighed.

"Okay, fine. I guess I'll check out a few pages."

Mrs. Reedy took the book, stamped a due date on it, and handed it back. I stared at it like it was a plate of fried slugs. Then I shoved it way in the bottom of my backpack, where no one could ever find it.

Not even me.

It is more impressive to whisper wisdom than it is to shout nonsense.

* * *

Many young people today feel like they must raise their voices to be heard. That is the opposite of the truth. Children of good manners will respond in a more positive fashion to those who speak in a measured tone, who feel no need to shout, because they're confident in the value of what they're saying.

Remember that the importance of what you're saying is not reflected in the volume of your voice.

I read a few pages of the book.

Then I read a few more.

Then a few more.

Before I knew it, I'd read practically *ten* pages.

Which, um, is a lot for me.

Hey, don't laugh. It's not like it was the first time I'd ever read a book or anything. I read a book at camp about a guy named Lech Walesa, who led a revolution and became president of Poland. He was cool and had an amazing mustache.

And I read *The Giving Tree* when I was about six. I loved that book. It was really, really short. And good! But mostly short.

This book was different than those two, though. *A Communication Guide for Boys and Girls* was one of those "how to be a better person" books that grown-ups were always reading. I wasn't really all that interested in how to be a better person, to be honest with you. I was completely satisfied with the person I was. Except for the girls thing.

So there I was, in the way, way back of the library, trying to get through the second chapter—Shy Is Not a Dirty Word—when I felt someone breathing over my shoulder. I turned around, and Emory was standing there. Emory was the kid from California who had swooped in and asked Eliza Collins to go out with him, even though the new kid asking out the prettiest girl breaks pretty much every rule in the middle school handbook.

The last thing I wanted was for him to see me reading a book on how to talk to girls—especially a chapter on shyness.

I stuffed the book into my backpack.

"What are you reading?" Emory asked.

"Some boring book."

Emory raised his eyebrows. "I heard you don't read *any* books. Ever."

"I don't. This is . . . to win a bet."

"Dude, I don't care if you read a whole library of books," he said. "I got other things on my mind."

"Like what?"

"Nah, I don't want to bother you with it," Emory said, even though he was pulling up a chair as he said it.

"It's cool." I was happy to hear about another guy's problems. It would probably make me feel a little better.

"This Eliza thing . . . it's freaking me out a little bit."

"Huh? What Eliza thing?"

Emory sighed a long, stressed-out, it's-hard-going-out-with-the-pretty-girl sigh. "Well, ever since we became boyfriend and girlfriend, it's like she's doing me this big favor," he explained. "I have to agree with everything she says, I have to laugh at all her jokes even when they're not that funny, she's the one who decides when and where we hang out—it's less like I'm her boyfriend and more like I'm her pet."

Pets! I immediately thought of Moose and Coco (my dogs) and how cute they were. But then I realized that they had nothing to do with this conversation.

"Dude," I said, trying to sound as California cool as possible. "That sounds like a major bummer."

"You know it, dude," Emory said. He sounded way more California cool than me, which made sense, since he was actually *from* California. "I just wish I knew how to talk to her about it. Saying stuff to girls can be such a nightmare."

Hey, wait a second.

"I know a thing or two about girls," I said. "Maybe I can help you out."

Emory looked confused. "Huh?"

"Hold on a second, I need to check something."

I turned my back on Emory, fished the book out of my backpack, flipped around until I found the page I was looking for, quickly scanned two paragraphs, then closed the book and put it back in my pack. All in about eighteen seconds.

"Dude, what was that about?" Emory asked.

"Oh, nothing." Then, totally casually, I added, "You know, uh, maybe you should try just, like, talking directly to her. Sometimes it's good to be direct with girls, even if it's a hard subject." I closed my eyes, trying to remember the rest. "And when you're saying something they don't want to hear, say it really calmly and quietly. That way, because you're being so low-key about it, she'll get defensive and start a fight."

Emory looked confused. "Huh?"

Oooops.

"I mean, *won't* get defensive and start a fight."

"Hmm," Emory said.

"It's true," I said. "Remember—it's more important to whisper wisdom than it is to shout nonsense."

Emory sat back in his chair and scratched his head for a while. Finally, he nodded.

"Dude, you are one smart dude," he said.

"Thanks, dude," I said.

Emory fist-bumped me, California style, and walked away. On his way out, he passed another kid and said, "Hey, that Charlie Joe is one smart dude."

I smiled.

Okay fine, I said to myself.

Maybe I'll read the rest of the book after all.

Spend as much time asking questions as you do answering them.

* * *

It is natural to be more interested in yourself than in anyone else. But you must always make an effort to pay attention to the person you're talking to. Be curious about his or her life, ask questions about his or her daily activities, and show a real interest in his or her answers.

Remember, you are having a CONVERSATION, not a MONOLOGUE.

At lunch, I had my second customer.

Big Phil Manning.

"Hey, Phil," I said, as he lumbered up to me. Phil was the strongest kid in our grade. He was voted "Most likely to become a mixed martial arts champion" in our yearbook. And the crazy thing was, he was going out with Celia Barbarossa, the fragile flute player who looked like she would lose a fight with a flower. But they'd happily been boyfriend and girlfriend for over two years, and we all assumed that we'd be going to their wedding some day.

Which is why I almost spit out a fish stick when Phil said, "I got girl trouble."

"Wait, what?"

"You heard me," Phil said. When he plopped down next to me with a THUNK! I could swear I felt the entire cafeteria shift just a little bit. "Girl trouble."

"What kind of girl trouble?"

"It's a long story. But Emory said you were the guy to talk to."

I scanned the room looking for Emory, but he was nowhere to be found. I didn't know whether to be mad or grateful. Sure, it was nice to be known as an expert on romance. But what if I gave Phil bad advice? It was entirely possible he'd pick me up and throw me like a football, all the way up to Canada.

"Um, I don't know about that," I said. "But . . . uh . . . what's the problem?"

Phil was about to say something when Pete and Timmy came up behind us and tossed their empty potato chip bags on my tray, for no other reason than to be annoying, which is as good a reason as any in middle school.

"Hey, can you throw those out for us?" Pete said.

"Yeah, that'd be sweet, Charlie Joe," Timmy added.

Phil stood up. "We're having a private conversation," he said, in his low voice.

I don't think I've ever seen two middle school kids scurry away faster.

Phil sat back down. "Where was I? Oh, yeah. So, Celia and me, we're like really into each other, you know?"

"Yeah, I know."

"But . . ." Phil stopped and scrunched up his face, as if what he was about to say caused him intense pain. "I think that as I get older and school gets harder and with football and everything, I think that maybe having a girlfriend might be too much of a distraction, you know? But I don't know if I should say anything to Celia."

"Huh," I said, which is probably not what a certified romanticologist would say.

As Phil stared at me—even his eyes had muscles—I broke out in a slight sweat. "So?" he pleaded. "What do you think?"

"I'm not sure."

"Come on, Charlie Joe! I've been worrying about this for like, forever! You gotta help me!"

Oh, jeez.

I closed my eyes, trying to think. In my mind, I went over the most recent pages of the book that I'd read, searching for something that would help. Do I say the same thing to Phil that I said to Emory? Do I try to come up with something new? Do I—

Suddenly I had it.

"Well, Phil," I said. "If there's one thing I know, it's that girls like to be treated as equals."

"What do you mean?"

"I mean, if this is a concern of yours, it might also be a concern of hers."

Phil frowned. "Huh," he said. "So what you're saying is, I should ask her if she's worried that I'm worried that having a girlfriend might get too distracting?"

"No," I said. "You should ask her if she's worried that having a boyfriend will be too distracting for *her*."

Phil didn't look too thrilled by that idea.

"I doubt she is," I said quickly. "But you never know. Just ask her. Then you can tell her that you're a little nervous about it, and see what she says. You guys can figure it out for sure. Seriously, it's no biggie. Once you talk about it you'll be fine."

Phil nodded, and I leaned in for the big finish. "Remember," I added thoughtfully, "it's a conversation, not a monologue."

Phil stared at me for about ten seconds without blinking. "Holy moly, Emory was right," he finally said. Then he slapped me on the back, which I was pretty sure would leave a mark. "You're a genius, Charlie Joe, anyone ever tell you that?"

"Not exactly, no."

"Well, you are. I gotta go find Celia."

He got up and left, which was my cue to leave, too. If Phil's conversation with Celia didn't go well, I sure as heck didn't want to be there to find out.

It turned out I had nothing to worry about.

Phil's conversation with Celia went REALLY well.

So did Emory's conversation with Eliza.

And the next thing I knew, I'd become the school's go-to guy on every boy-girl problem that came up.

It usually happened at lunch and recess; I'd be sitting there, minding my own business, when some kid would come up to me with that look in his eye: a combination of nervousness, embarrassment, and desperation.

"Take a seat," I'd say. And they would.

Timmy started calling me "The Love Doctor." He had a point. I should have opened an office and charged by the hour. I would have made way more money than I did with that whole dog-walking thing. (Don't ask.)

I had no idea there were so many different kinds of boy-girl problems in middle school! But the funny thing was, most of them had nothing to do with boys and girls who were actually boyfriend and girlfriend. Usually, it had to do with some guy who liked a girl but was too shy to say so; or sometimes, some kid had heard that a girl liked him, but he didn't know how to tell the girl that he didn't like her back. My advice to these people almost always boiled down to a simple sentence that was on page twenty-four of the book:

A quick conversation is better than a lifetime of regret.

They would nod thoughtfully, just like Phil did, and go try their luck at being honest.

It was kind of fun being the school love guru, to tell you the truth. By the time I finished reading *A Communication Guide for Boys and Girls* a week later—hold your applause, please—it seemed like even the teachers were ready to ask me for dating advice. There was no romantic problem I couldn't solve.

Except one.

"Got a minute?"

I was coming out of drama class, on my way to P.E. where I would be busy avoiding participating in gymnastics, when she cornered me.

Hannah Spivero.

Now, Hannah and I go way back. I first met her in kindergarten, but I didn't actually develop a crush on her until, oh, let's see . . . about two hours later. But the good news is, the crush didn't last that long. Only about seven years.

So yeah, let's just say that I spent a lot of days, weeks, months, and years waiting for Hannah to come up to me and say, "Got a minute?"

So when it actually happened, what did I say?

"Not really."

She looked shocked, for good reason. "What do you mean, not really?"

"I mean, if I'm not out on that balance beam in the next four minutes, Mr. Radonski is going to make me do laps for the next four hours."

Mr. Radonski, by the way, is the gym teacher. He makes marine drill sergeants look like yoga instructors.

"This will only take a minute," Hannah said.

She seemed kind of upset. I weighed my options: Risk the wrath of Radonski, or leave the one-and-only Hannah Spivero standing there, looking sad.

I decided to take my chances.

"What's up?"

"It's about Jake."

I should have known! Of course it was about Jake! The whole school was counting on me to solve their boy-girl problems, so why should Hannah be any different? Especially since Jake was one of my best friends, and she probably figured I could offer extra insight.

I sighed, extra loudly. "What about him?"

"I think he likes someone else," Hannah said. Then she started to cry.

I stopped sighing immediately. *Whoa.* This was big. This was potentially life-changing. For everyone involved.

"That's impossible," I said. "Jake is like completely crazy about you." *A feeling I'm familiar with*, I could have added, but didn't.

Hannah shook her head. "I thought so, too," she said, sniffling. "But that was before this morning. I was waiting outside his math class, like I always do, but he didn't come out. I figured maybe he was talking with Mr. Westfall, talking about some incredibly complicated theorem or something, you know, since he's such a math genius. But then Mr. Westfall came out, too, and Jake was still in there. So

34

I went inside, and he was sitting at his desk, writing something. He was concentrating so hard he didn't even see me coming. So I went up to him and said, 'Hi.' He looked shocked and quickly put away what he was writing, but before he did, I could see a little bit of what he wrote."

"What did it say?"

Hannah blew her nose.

"'*I know you're worried about Hannah, but please don't be. I love you.*'"

Oooooof. That was bad.

"Huh," I said, trying to sound casual. "Did you ask him what it was?"

Hannah choked out a laugh. "Are you kidding? I said I had to go, and I ran out of there. I didn't want him to see me totally lose it." She wiped her eyes and looked at her phone. "I'm sorry, Charlie Joe. I just thought . . . you know, since you're so good about this kind of stuff . . . you might have an idea about what I should do."

Now, call me crazy, but I was pretty sure there wasn't anything in *A Communication Guide for Boys and Girls* about what to say to the girl that you've had a crush on for most of your life when she tells you that her boyfriend likes someone else. No wait—make that *loves* someone else.

So I did what anyone in my situation would have done.

I stalled.

"Um . . . well, let me at least talk to Jake about it . . . I'm sure there's a perfectly reasonable explanation . . .

um . . . you're like the greatest person in the world and so there's no way that Jake doesn't like you anymore . . . that's crazy . . . you're like the most awesome person in the world—"

I stopped talking because I felt two arms suddenly wrap themselves around me.

They were Hannah's.

"Oh, Charlie Joe," she said. "You've always been so incredibly sweet to me. I know it's been a little awkward for us over the last few years—"

"That's not true," I interrupted, even though it totally was.

"Well, either way," Hannah said. "Thank you for being there for me. I don't know what I'd do without you."

She was still hugging me—actually, it was more like clinging to me—and I gently patted her on the back. We stayed like that for what seemed like a week, but was probably only about eight seconds. I had no idea what to do. Finally, she pulled away a little bit and looked up at me. Her eyes were wide and a little red. Then she smiled. It was like she was waiting for me to do something. Or, more like, she was giving me *permission* to do something.

And I was pretty sure I knew what that something was.

I thought for a second. If it was ever going to happen, this was probably the one chance I would get. And hey, I didn't have a girlfriend, and her boyfriend was in love with someone else, so why not?

I closed my eyes, and the next thing I knew, I kissed her. I think it might have even lasted like six seconds.

Seven years of waiting, for six seconds of heaven. It was totally worth it!

Until everything else happened.

About two seconds into my six-second kiss with Hannah Spivero, I thought I heard the door open. I decided to ignore it.

First mistake.

At the four-second mark, I heard a backpack rustle. Then, at six seconds, an incredibly familiar voice:

"Oh, sorry! I didn't realize anyone was in here."

I turned my head and saw her.

Katie Friedman.

She looked—well, what's the word that describes *shock times ten*?

Hannah and I immediately stopped kissing and stared at Katie. She stared back. No one moved.

Finally, Hannah whispered, "I'm really sorry," and ran out of the room.

That left the two of us. I decided I had to say something.

I went with, "Katie."

She suddenly looked at the ground. "Charlie Joe, you don't have to say anything. I know how long you've liked Hannah. That's great. Although isn't she still going out with Jake?"

"That's just it," I mumbled. "He's . . . um . . . it's complicated."

"Well, it's none of my business!" Katie said brightly. "I'm really happy for you! Well, I have to go."

"Katie, wait."

But she didn't wait. She bent down to pick up her backpack, and as she stood up, her eyes locked on mine.

"Katie," I said, for the third time in thirty seconds.

"See you, Charlie Joe." And she was gone.

As I watched her go, my heart did a weird little somersault. And that was the moment I realized something I'd probably known for a long time but hadn't been able to fully admit—to myself, or anyone else.

The girl I was crazy about wasn't Hannah Spivero after all.

It was Katie Friedman.

I stood there alone with my thoughts for about ten more seconds, until I did the only thing that was left to do.

Go to gym.

I was late, of course. Mr. Radonski looked furious. He also looked delighted that he was able to direct that fury at me.

"JACKSON!"

"Yes, Mr. Radonski?"

"This is inexcusable!"

You're late!

"I know, Mr. Radonski. I'm really sorry."

"REALLY SORRY DOESN'T CUT IT! DO FOUR LAPS!"

I was actually relieved, because four laps around the gym is a lot better than trying to do the parallel bars, if you ask me.

I was just getting started when I saw Jake out of the corner of my eye. At first I felt a little nervous seeing him, since I'd kissed his girlfriend. Then I remembered he'd broken his girlfriend's heart. He was the one who should be nervous.

"Jake?"

He was staring at the ground, like he was either trying to do a cartwheel or looking for a dropped contact lens. He looked up and squinted, which is when I realized it was the dropped-contact-lens option.

"Oh, hey, Charlie Joe."

"Run with me for a minute, I want to ask you something."

"I can't! I'm supposed to be doing cartwheels."

Wait a second. Was he doing cartwheels or looking for his contact lens? I decided not to care.

"Radonski is way over there. Come on, I have something important to ask you."

Jake thought for a second, then apparently decided that doing a half-decent cartwheel was a lost cause. He shrugged and started jogging along. We were both out of breath after about eight steps. Pathetic, I know.

"What did you . . . want to ask me . . ."

"Well . . . it's about . . . Hannah . . ."

Jake stopped. So I stopped.

"What about her?"

I pulled Jake underneath the rings. We looked up and saw Eliza Collins hanging upside down, her long blond hair dangling so low we could practically touch it. She looked very graceful. Also, very brave. I'm scared of heights so I got a doctor's note that dismissed me from rings. Doctor's notes really work! You should try it sometime.

"What about Hannah?" Jake repeated.

"Um . . ." I wasn't quite sure how to bring it up. "She . . . uh . . . said you were writing some note or something at the end of math today?"

Jake suddenly looked incredibly embarrassed. Wow. So it was true! He really DID like another girl!

"She saw that?"

I nodded. "Yup."

"Oh, man," Jake said. "I really didn't want her to see that. She's going to give me such a hard time."

"Ya think?" I snorted. "That's like, the understatement of the year. What were you thinking?"

"It's not that bad," Jake said. "A lot of kids do it."

"No they don't!"

"Well," Jake said, shaking his head, "then they should. And I'm not going to feel bad just because I did."

I couldn't believe it. Who *was* this kid? Was he a body

snatcher? What happened to the nice, respectful, responsible, in-love-with-Hannah Jake Katz that I knew?

"I can't believe what you're saying," I said, finally.

Jake turned, his eyes blazing, and whacked me on the shoulder. "Seriously, Charlie Joe? You're going to make *me* feel bad? I know everyone thinks she's a little crazy and obnoxious, and she thinks that Hannah and I are way too young to be boyfriend and girlfriend, but so what! She still deserves a birthday card! She's my mom! And I love her and want to tell her what a great mom she is! SO SUE ME!"

Uh-oh.

I stared in shock. "Your MOM?!"

"Yes! Now just leave me alone!"

As Jake ran off, I thought about the fact that I'd just kissed my friend's girlfriend, and all he'd done was tell his mother he loved her.

I suddenly felt about zero feet tall.

How was I able to give everyone else such great advice but still manage to get myself in a huge mess?

The good news was that Mr. Radonski gave me ten more laps to think about it.

Hey Katie

**

Katie are you there?

**

Why aren't you returning any of my texts?

**

Are you mad at me?

**

If you're mad I'd rather you just said so

**

Fine be that way

Okay, so texting wasn't getting me anywhere.

I waited for Katie after school by the blacktop, before the buses (or the moms) came.

When she saw me, she stopped in her tracks for one quick second, then smiled and kept walking toward me.

"Hey, Charlie Joe!" she said. Her voice was bright, but her eyes were far away.

"Hey."

She looked past me. "Um, I'm kind of in a rush, I've got rehearsal today and stuff . . ."

She was talking about her band, CHICKMATE—they are really good.

"Do you guys have a gig coming up?"

She kind of laughed a little. "Since when are you interested in my music career, Charlie Joe?"

"Since always!"

"Yeah, right."

She looked like she really wanted to go, so I got right to the point.

"I've been texting you."

Katie made sure her eyes landed anywhere but on my face. "You were? Yeah, um, well, you know I'm not that

45

into texting." It's true, she wasn't. In fact, earlier in the year, she convinced a bunch of other kids to give up their phones for a whole week just to see if they could do it. Needless to say, I didn't participate.

"Oh, okay," I said. "I just . . . wanted to, you know, say hi."

"We're not supposed to have our phones on in class . . . so, yeah . . . well, I gotta go."

I gave up, and said nothing. She started to leave, then turned back.

"Tell Moose and Coco I say hi," she said. "Give them a kiss for me."

Katie had always loved my dogs, which made me feel just a tiny, tiny bit better.

At least she still liked someone in my family.

You know what the great thing about dogs is? They don't judge. They don't blame. They don't yell, or pretend to be nice to you when they're really, really mad at you. They just love you. (As long as you feed them delicious treats.)

Which is why Moose and Coco were both dining on small pieces of sausage while I was telling them the whole story.

"And I felt like such a jerk," I was saying, "standing there, kissing Hannah, when Katie was the one I really liked all along! Can you believe that, you guys?"

They looked up at me, chomping away. They didn't say anything, but I could tell they totally understood.

I was about to get them a few crackers to top off their midday snack when my mom and Megan got home.

"Stop feeding the dogs human food," Megan said. "They're going to get spoiled and fat."

"You're going to get spoiled and fat," I answered.

"That's enough, you two," said my mom. It was her goal in life to make sure Megan and I treated each other with complete love and respect twenty-four hours a day, three hundred sixty-five days a year. Gotta love moms.

"Where were you guys?" I asked. Usually I kind of liked it when no one was home, but today, I felt like I wanted some company.

"Ugh," Megan said.

"SAT prep," my mom clarified.

Megan rolled her eyes. "Like I said, ugh."

"Yikes," I added.

As impossible as it seemed, Megan was getting started on the whole college process. That meant tests, applications, essays, interviews, and most of all, pressure.

I'm in no rush for any of that stuff. No rush at *all*.

"What are you doing home?" my mom asked me. "Weren't you supposed to go to Jake's house after school today?"

She was right, I was. But after our conversation during gym, I realized I didn't really deserve to be his friend right then. I'd kissed his girlfriend! And all he'd done wrong was tell his mom that he loved her.

So I'd told Jake at the end of school that I wasn't feeling well.

"Jake forgot he had to do something," I lied to my mom.

As soon as my mom walked away, I texted Hannah.

Hey I looked for you after school. I need to tell you the deal with Jake!

Two seconds later, I got a text back.

Jake and I talked, he told me everything! Then I told him what happened.

Gulp.

Was he mad? I texted back.

He was at first but now everything's fine. Stupid misunderstanding! Sorry about today. I hope you're okay. Thanks again for listening.

I texted back.

Okay.

I left out the part about realizing how I liked Katie and then messed it up forever, at exactly the same time.

After cereal, I played a few video games by myself, but that wasn't much fun, so I went up to my room. I lay down on the bed, trying to figure out what to do next—not just that day, but with my life—when I glanced over and saw the book lying there on the night table.

A Communication Guide for Boys and Girls.

Communicating with girls is overrated, I said to myself. But I picked up the book anyway and opened to a random page. The first words I saw were these:

You will never know the answer, if you don't ask the question.

And that's when I made the decision.

I was going to do exactly that.

I was going to tell Katie everything.

Be direct!

* * *

Many children find it hard to communicate directly with members of the opposite sex. Because of nerves, or fear of rejection, they prefer to connect by other means: through other people, perhaps, or by passing notes.

This is not productive.

If you want to pursue a friendship with a boy or girl, or even possibly a romantic relationship, the proper way to act is by asking directly. He or she will have no choice but to answer in a similarly direct fashion, and you will have established a pattern of honesty and respect.

Do not be afraid.

Remember:

You will never know the answer, if you don't ask the question.

Part Two
PERSONAL HEROES

So guess what? Once people found out that I was writing this book on girls, I started getting a lot of phone calls. It turns out that everyone thinks they're some kind of expert on romance, and, of course, they all want to put their two cents in. So, just to get them off my back, I agreed to let some people offer their own advice on romance. Don't worry, I gave them very strict rules—the first of which was, be quick about it. Anyway, you'll see them scattered throughout this book. Do me a favor and read them. If you don't, I'll never hear the end of it.

Timmy McGibney's Guide to Romance

TWO WORDS: HAIR GEL

To me, there's one thing that's more important than anything else if you want to be irresistible to the ladies.

The hair's gotta be working.

For me, it's all about the hair gel. Throw a little on in the morning, make the hair a little spiky to show a little confidence, and then you're ready to roll. Think about the attitude. If you treat yourself like the real deal, that's how the girls will treat you, too.

And if that doesn't work, then just buy them stuff.

"**Hey, Katie. Listen,** I have something I have to say to you. I've been meaning to tell you this for a long time. You know how I liked Hannah, like, forever? And then, I liked Zoe, but she moved away? And you know how I used to talk about all that stuff with you, and you were so nice and helpful about it? And you know how then you went out with Nareem, and that was great, but then you decided that maybe you didn't like him that way anymore? Well, guess what? I think I know why I don't have a girlfriend and you don't have a boyfriend. I think it's because maybe deep down, we both know the truth. We both know what's really happening here. Don't you agree?"

I waited for the answer for a long time, but none came.

Maybe that's because mirrors can't talk.

* * *

That's right, I was talking to the mirror.

What? You expected me to just waltz over to her house and sweep her off her feet, like in some movie?

Well, sorry. Real life doesn't work that way.

So, yeah, I was in the bathroom, practicing. I was

planning on talking to Katie in school the next morning, and I wanted to be prepared. I figured I had only one shot at this thing, and I didn't want to blow it.

I was halfway through my third rehearsal when there was a knock on the door.

More like a bang, actually.

BANG! BANG! BANG!

"What are you doing in there?" Megan yelled from outside. "I need to get my hairbrush!"

"One minute," I yelled.

"I'll give you three seconds," she said, and she wasn't exaggerating. Three seconds later, more banging.

"Fine!"

I opened the door, and she ran in, grabbed the brush, and ran out.

"What's your problem?" I shouted after her.

"You are!" she shouted back.

I followed her back into her room, where at least seven books were spread out in front of her.

"Seriously, what is your problem?"

"Finals," she said, typing on her laptop with one hand and combing her hair with the other. "Finals are my problem."

Whenever my sister gets nervous she combs her hair, and finals—short for final exams—make everyone nervous. Even my incredibly smart sister. I think it might be the most dreaded word in all of high school.

In any case, a room with seven books spread out in it was no place for a person like me. I started to leave quietly.

"Charlie Joe, you have no idea how lucky you are."

Right that minute, I wasn't feeling all that lucky. "What do you mean?"

"I mean," Megan said, "that you're still a kid. You don't have to worry about any of this stuff. Finals, colleges, school. I mean, think about it. Your grades don't even count!"

That stopped me in my tracks. My grades don't *count*? How could that be possible? My parents had been after me to get good grades since before I was born.

"Hold on a second. What are you talking about?"

Megan rolled her eyes. "Everyone knows that they don't start keeping track of your GPA until high school."

"Who's 'they'? And what's a GPA?"

"'They' are the colleges. And 'GPA' stands for grade point average. Why do you think I'm killing myself with all this stuff? Colleges are all about your GPA and test scores. But none of that matters for you."

"Why not?"

"Because you're not in high school yet!" Megan snapped. "All I can say is, enjoy your little middle school life with your little middle school problems while you still can."

I wanted to get out of there before she got so stressed out she threw her hairbrush at me, but I had to make sure I heard her correctly. "Wait a second. You mean, because I'm in middle school, my grades don't matter at all in terms of college and stuff?"

She nodded jealously. "Yup, you little worm. You can get A's or C's—it's all the same."

Wow! Things were definitely looking up.

Then she sighed and pointed at her huge pile of books. "But don't worry, my little friend—someday soon, all this will be yours."

She picked up a book and started to read, which was my cue to leave.

Someday soon, maybe.

But not yet.

As soon as I got to school the next day, I knew word was out that I kissed Hannah Spivero.

I could tell because all the kids I didn't know very well looked at me as if I was the coolest kid on earth, and all of my friends looked at me as if I was the worst kid on earth.

Jake was first.

"I don't want to talk to you right now," he said, when he saw me coming.

"Jake—"

"Stop. I know what happened, and I just don't want to talk about it."

"Well, I'm really, really sorry. Hannah was really upset. Please don't blame her."

Jake glanced up at me, and I could see the hurt in his eyes. "I don't," he said. "I blame you."

I got similar treatment from everyone else in the gang: Timmy, Eliza, Nareem, even the new kid, Emory, whom I'd given advice to about Eliza. Talk about ungrateful!

I didn't get similar treatment from Katie, though, because I didn't get *any* treatment from Katie. She just kept smiling that fake smile at me, which was way worse than if she'd yelled at me, to tell you the truth.

Hannah was the only one who was a little nice to me, because I think she felt a little guilty and knew it wasn't *all* my fault. But she was way more concerned with making Jake feel better than she was with making me feel better, and I couldn't blame her for that.

And then there was Pete.

Pete Milano—the most obnoxious, irritating kid in the whole school, but still somehow a good friend of mine—was the only one who acted normal to me. But that's how Pete is. He just wants to have a good time, and he doesn't judge. I guess he's kind of like a dog that way.

I sat next to Pete in Social Studies. Usually he drove me crazy, but today, I was just grateful to have someone to talk to. (Really quietly, since you're not supposed to talk in class.)

"Hey, Pete," I whispered.

"Yeah?"

"Thanks for not being mad at me like everyone else."

"Why would I be mad? It's not like you kissed my girl-friend. And by the way, if you ever do kiss Mareli, I will punch you in the worst place on your body to get punched. I think you know where I'm talking about."

Note to self: Never kiss Mareli.

It seemed like a good time to change the subject. "Hey, Pete, did you know our grades don't matter until we get to high school?"

"Cool!" Pete seemed excited by the news, but I'm not sure why. I was pretty sure he was going to get the exact same grades in high school that he was getting now. Bad ones.

"Mr. Jackson, Mr. Milano, I'll thank you to hold your tongues," said Ms. Albone, our teacher.

Pete actually started holding his tongue. "Oww, it hurtsth," he wailed, laughing.

"Sorry, Ms. Albone," I said.

Pete winked at me and said way too loudly, "Grades don't count in middle school, remember? You said!"

"*Shhh!*" I hissed, but I was too late—Ms. Albone was walking over to my desk.

Oh, great.

"Did you really say that, Charlie Joe? That grades don't count in middle school?"

"I—can't remember."

She shook her head sadly and headed back to the front of the classroom. "As I was saying," she said, "for our last big assignment of the year, I'm asking students to write a five-page paper on anyone they consider to be a personal hero. They can be alive or dead, young or old, male or female. It's totally up to you. But you have to make a very convincing case why they're your hero. This will rely on everything we've learned this year about how to state a point of view clearly, and then how to back it up with examples and research."

Ugh.

A five-page paper.

I was going to have to use some pretty big margins.

Jill Farnak's hand went up in the front row. "Um, Ms. Albone? Is it okay if the hero is a friend?"

"Well," Ms. Albone said, "you have to really believe they're a hero. They can't just be heroic because they're your friend."

Jill looked crushed. "Okay."

63

A few more kids asked questions, but my admittedly limited attention span had just about run out. I started thinking about everything that had happened over the last couple of days. I was exhausted. So much had gone wrong, and now I had to worry about a five-page paper! But there were a few good things to remember. At least we had camp reunion weekend coming up. At least Katie was still talking to me, even if it was just fake talk about the dogs. And at least I knew that my grades still didn't really count. If only I could figure out a way to avoid doing any real research . . .

I raised my hand.

"Excuse me, Ms. Albone? Is it okay if the person is a family member?"

Ms. Albone smiled. "Well, I'd have to say yes to that one. It's perfectly acceptable if you decide to write about someone in your own family. I'm sure they would be very honored! Although, I would prefer not to get twenty-four papers about your mothers and fathers."

Yes! As far as I knew, there were no biographies yet written about anybody in my family. Which meant, I didn't have to read any.

So which member of my family should I write about?

I looked across the room and saw Katie, taking notes like she always did. I still had my big speech I wanted to give her. When was I going to do it? What was she going to say? She was probably going to laugh at me. A speech wasn't going to do it. I had to prove myself some other way. I had to show her who I really was—a decent person. I had to—

"Charlie Joe? Are you even listening to me?"

"Sorry, Ms. Albone."

She clucked her tongue in that disapproving teacher-y way. "I was just saying, no matter who you all decide to do your paper on, you still need to do some real research. No short cuts."

"Yes, Ms. Albone."

No short cuts.

I was starting to realize how true that was.

In school, and in life.

Eliza Collins's
Guide to Romance

IT'S ALL ABOUT THE PERSONALITY

Yes, it's fun being beautiful. I really like it. But if you ask me, it doesn't mean anything unless you're a really nice person. Boys don't want to go out with girls who are mean. They don't want to go out with girls who are super bossy. And they definitely don't want to go out with girls who treat them badly. Take it from me. Be nice, and nice things will happen to you!

Oh, and also, wear colors that complement your skin tone. That's really important, too.

"You again?"

"Hi, Mrs. Reedy. I'm back."

It's true. I was back in the library for the second time in less than a month. I couldn't believe it, either.

"What can I do for you, Charlie Joe?"

I looked at her and waited.

"No funny cracks about what I'm doing here?"

Mrs. Reedy smiled. "Charlie Joe, I've worked in various libraries over half my life. I've seen plenty of kids who hate reading way more than you. But some of them—not all, but some—come into the library one day, for one reason or another, and they find a book they like. Then, eventually, some of those kids come back and they find another book they like. And again. And before you know it, they're some of my best customers." She smiled. "I'm not saying you'll be one of my regulars anytime soon. But let's put it this way: I'm not as shocked to see you as I was a few days ago. And I'll be even less shocked if I see you in here again in a few days."

"Let's not get crazy," I said. "I'm just here to return the book."

She laughed. "Not getting crazy."

I handed her *A Communication Guide for Boys and Girls*. "What did you think?" she asked.

"Well, to tell you the truth," I said, "that book got me in a lot of trouble."

"Uh-oh."

"Yup. Now I need a book called *A Communication Guide for a Boy Who Really Likes a Girl, Even Though She Totally Hates Him Back*."

"I don't think I have that one," said Mrs. Reedy.

As she checked the book back in, I heard a familiar voice in the hall.

Uh-oh.

I turned to get the heck out of there, but before I could make my escape, I felt a very tall person behind me.

"Hello, Mr. Jackson."

I turned around. "Oh, hi, Mrs. Sleep! Very nice to see you! Well, I gotta go."

Mrs. Sleep was the principal of our school, so it was my sworn duty to spend as little time in her presence as possible. Nothing good ever came out of our conversations. But today, I was in the library! How bad could it be?

"Mr. Jackson," she said in her deep, scary voice (I think all principals have deep, scary voices), "do you believe that the middle school education is of a certain value, to children such as yourself?"

Was this a trick question?

"Of course I do, Mrs. Sleep! Education is the most important thing in life! It helps prepare us for high school, and then for college, and besides, education is the best way to make sure we go on to have successful careers and become responsible citizens."

Phew! Bullet dodged.

I started to walk away, but Mrs. Sleep cleared her throat, which was code for *I'm not done with you yet*.

"Just one more thing."

She looked down on me, her glasses dangling on the tip of her nose.

"Did you, or did you not, mention in Ms. Albone's class that grades in middle school don't count?"

Oh, *that*.

"I—I—"

Mrs. Sleep put her hand on my shoulder, which feels very different from when, say, Katie Friedman puts her hand on my shoulder.

"Mr. Jackson. We've been friends a long time." (*Friends?*) "And I really feel like we've made a great deal of progress over these last few years. So it pains me to hear these things."

I had nothing to say, so I just waited for her to finish. *Prayed* for her to finish, is more like it.

"I know you have your research paper coming up in Ms. Albone's class. You can prove to me that you take your studies seriously by presenting an excellent report. Can you do that for me, Mr. Jackson?"

"Absolutely, Mrs. Sleep."

"Good." She pushed her glasses up on her nose and bent down so we were eye to eye. "Because if you don't, you may be enjoying recess inside with me for the rest of the year, discussing the value of a middle-school education."

And with *that*, Mrs. Sleep nodded at me, nodded at Mrs. Reedy, turned on her heels, and walked away.

Mrs. Reedy looked at me with disappointment in her eyes. "'Grades don't count?' Charlie Joe, that's a silly thing to say. Even for you."

Ugh. There were so many ways to answer that—it was Megan's fault for telling me that in the first place, it was Pete's fault for saying it out loud in class, it was Mrs. Albone's fault for telling on me—but, instead, I decided to be a man about it and avoid the subject altogether.

"Have a nice weekend," I said, and I left the library.

Hopefully for the last time.

So, there was bad news and good news.

The bad news was, I liked a girl who had just seen me kiss a different girl, half my friends were mad at me, I might have to spend recess with my principal for the rest of the year, and I had a five-page paper due in a week.

The good news was, it was time to forget all that, because I was on a train heading into New York City!

The last time I was in the city, it was to visit my dad's office, where we had a fun day, except for the part where I almost got him fired. But that was before I taught his boss how to use the mouse on his computer and ended up saving my dad's job!

Which he's never thanked me for, by the way.

This time, I was heading in for Rithubukkee Reunion Weekend, and I couldn't wait. I was really excited to see my friends from camp: George Feedleman, Jack Strong, Lauren Rubin, and all the rest. I was even excited to see Ms. Domerca, my teacher, who was amazing even though she dressed like a color-blind toddler.

Nareem was going to be there, since he went to the camp, too. And you know who else was going to be there?

Yeah. Her. Initials K.F.

So I guess I wasn't leaving *all* my troubles behind.

My dad decided not to go—I believe his exact words were, "I wouldn't go into the city on a weekend if it had the last chocolate chip cookie on earth"—so it was my mom and I who got on the train. My mom immediately passed out. It's amazing how she can fall asleep in a split second. Sometimes we'll be watching TV, and I'll say to her, "This show is good," and she'll say, "I know!" and I'll say, "Who's your favorite character?" and she'll be asleep.

The train ride was about an hour, but it seemed like ten hours. I spent most of the time texting Timmy and Pete about absolutely nothing.

Then I decided to text Jake.

`Hey, I know you're still mad about that whole thing with Hannah and I totally get it. Like I said I'm really sorry. I hope we can get back to normal really soon.`

That's the good thing about texting. You can say things you would never actually say.

But he didn't text me back. Which is the bad thing about texting.

Finally, the guy came on the loudspeaker and said, "Next stop, Grand Central Terminal." I got all excited and looked out the window, but then I remembered we were in a tunnel, so I closed my eyes and imagined the city, just waiting there for me, with buildings so tall you could stick your hand out a window and touch a cloud.

Then a guy who just *had* to get off the train first whacked me on the head with his backpack as he headed to the door. I remembered I was about to go where people are *not* messing around. This was the big city, baby.

Nine endless minutes later, I nudged my mom. "We're here. Wake up! We're here."

She opened her eyes groggily, stretched her arms high above her head, and said, "Already?"

Did I mention that the reception for the reunion was at the New York Public Library?

If I didn't, it's probably because I tried to block out that part.

On the brochure announcing the reunion weekend, it said, "The New York Public Library holds more than 53 million books and other items."

Just knowing that there were 53 million books *on earth* made a small patch of hives break out in my brain.

After we dropped our stuff at the hotel—which I thought was really nice, but my mom said was "so totally not worth the price"—we walked through Times Square to the library. Have you ever been to Times Square? If not, imagine the busiest part of your downtown. Now multiply it by 50 million. You literally cannot walk more than a foot in Times Square without bumping into one person, being handed a piece of paper by another person, being asked to pose for a picture by a third person who is dressed as a cartoon character, while listening to loud music being played by four more people who set up their instruments right on the street. And also, no one waits for the light to turn green. NO ONE. As soon as there's an inch of day-light between cars, people make a break for it. Except me and Mom.

We were waiting patiently for one light to change, with people a little annoyed because we were in their way, when I said, "Can we go?"

"Absolutely not," said my mom. "That's dangerous. And illegal."

So we just stood there. We might as well have written OUT-OF-TOWN LOSERS on our foreheads.

Finally we made it to Forty-Second Street and Fifth Avenue. We looked up and saw what looked like the hugest mansion ever built. I couldn't believe it was a library! Outside the main entrance, there were two amazingly cool

lion statues. I wasn't sure what lions had to do with reading books, except that they're both scary.

My mom stared up at the library in awe. "Wow, that is one gorgeous building."

"I know," I said, shaking my head. "What a shame."

"Charlie Joe! About time!"

We'd been in the library for approximately five seconds when I heard someone call my name. I looked up and saw a giant person running toward me like a goofy gazelle. It took me a minute to realize who it was—and once I did, it made perfect sense.

"George?"

The goofy gazelle teetered to a stop in front of me. "Yup! Can you believe it?"

George Feedleman was the camp genius and one of my best pals there. He was also the camp giant, and it looked like he'd grown another two feet.

"Wow, George. You're . . . you're huge."

"Thanks!" George exclaimed. "I made the travel basketball team! Thanks to you making me play at camp!"

I quickly scanned my memory to evaluate George's basketball skills and came to the immediate conclusion that his travel team couldn't have been very good.

George pulled my arm. "Come see the guys!"

I waved goodbye to my mom, who had already started chatting with some other parents, and followed George. It seemed like the reception was taking place right there in the main hallway, because there were chairs and tables set up, a podium with a microphone, and a huge table filled with snacks and chips and drinks. We walked all the way down to the far end of the table, where there were a bunch of kids hanging around, laughing and smiling and chomping on cookies.

"Hey, everyone," I said.

They all turned around: Jack Strong, Eric Cunkler, Jeremy Kim, and Sam Thurber, from my cabin; this girl Becky, who was one of Eric's good friends at camp; and Nareem.

And Katie.

"Charlie Joe!!" Jack yelled.

Then it was a blur of hugs and high-fives, as we all greeted each other like we were returning from a war.

The only one who didn't jump up to say hi was Katie. I went over to her. "Are you going to ignore me here, too?"

She gave me that irritatingly polite smile. "What are you talking about?"

And for the first time since I kissed Hannah, I stopped feeling guilty and started feeling annoyed. "Whatever." I headed over to the snack table and was just about to put the first of many chocolate chip cookies into my mouth when someone came up from behind me and squeezed me like I was an orange and they were really thirsty for juice.

It could only be one person.

I turned around. "Dwayne!"

Dwayne was my counselor at camp, and he was an awesome guy, when he liked you. When he was mad at you, though, he was quite possibly the scariest person on earth. Luckily, he liked me about 77 percent of the time.

"Hey, little man," he said. "Good to see you." He looked me up and down. "Looking a little scrawny, though. What happened to those push-ups I had you doing?"

"Oh right, those," I said. "I think I left them at camp. I can't find them."

Dwayne laughed, which sounded like a lion roaring. "HA! I've missed that sense of humor. So, how's your year been goin'?"

"Decent, I guess."

Dwayne looked disappointed. "That's all you're gonna give me? Come on CJ, you're always good for a story or two! Still avoiding schoolwork like the plague? How many detentions have you had? How 'bout girls—you killin' it with the ladies?"

I snuck a look at Katie, who was busy not sneaking a look at me. "Actually, the opposite, kind of," I told Dwayne. "Everyone at school has a girlfriend except me."

Dwayne looked shocked. "Seriously? Dude, that's nuts. I always thought you were the man with the MOVES!"

"All out of moves, I guess."

"Well, don't you worry," Dwayne said. "You just keep playing your game. You'll be fine." Dwayne gave me another high-five and walked away, leaving me to wonder what he meant by *playing my game*. I thought the whole point was to just be yourself. Ugh! This whole girls thing is a nightmare.

"Read any good books lately?" said a voice behind me.

I turned around to see Ms. Domerca standing there. Of all the teachers at camp—the camp called them "workshop leaders," but don't be fooled, they were teachers—Ms.

Domerca was my favorite. She was nice, she was funny, and she didn't make me feel bad for not liking reading and writing.

She was a pretty unusual dresser, though. Today, she was all snazzed up for the reception—meaning she was wearing a yellow and white shirt, a purple skirt, a tie with orange flowers on it, and a blue tuxedo jacket.

We hugged, and my hair got caught on one of her seven necklaces.

"It's great to see you," I said.

She stepped back and looked at me. "Are you sure about that? You don't look all that thrilled. What's wrong? All your pals are here, but you look like you just ate some bad fish."

That sounded disgusting, but I knew what she meant. "No, I'm good. It's a little strange to see everyone again, that's all."

"Well, reunions are always strange at first, but they only stay that way for about ten seconds," Ms. Domerca said. "Then they get awesome. Have fun!" And she went to greet some other kids and their parents.

George came galloping back over, this time with Cathy Ruddy by his side. Cathy was an adorable girl with bright red hair, and she was George's camp girlfriend. Judging by the way they were gazing into each other's eyes, she was his noncamp girlfriend, too.

"Cathy made it!" George said, lovingly.

"Hey, Charlie Joe!" Cathy said. "It is so great to see you!"

"Thanks, Cathy," I said. "You, too."

Cathy blazed her blue eyes at me. "Where's Katie? Is Nareem here? Are they still going out? Do you still like her?"

Jeez, that was fast.

I glared at George, and he started examining his glass of punch very carefully.

"Whoever said anything about me liking Katie?"

Cathy laughed. "Everyone knows you like Katie," she said, as if it were the most obvious thing in the world.

And that was when I stopped thinking and just started blabbing.

"I don't get why everyone is so convinced I like Katie. That's like the dumbest thing I ever heard. We're friends. We've always been friends, and we'll always be friends. But that's it. As if I would ever like Katie! That's like liking your sister. Gross."

But George and Cathy weren't looking at me. They were looking past me, and I suddenly realized exactly what they were looking at.

I turned around and saw Katie, standing there, frozen in place.

She'd heard every word.

"Oh, hey," I said. "I didn't see you there."

She didn't say anything. I felt bad, but I couldn't feel guilty. I was tired of feeling guilty.

"What?" I said. "Isn't that what you want? You barely even talk to me anymore."

She shot daggers at me with her eyes. "Maybe if you weren't too busy kissing other girls, you'd actually have a clue what I want," she hissed. Then she turned on her heels and walked away.

"That's not fair! I tried to apologize, but you wouldn't give me the chance!" I shouted after her, but she didn't turn around.

"Jeez," George said. "Should we go get some punch?" But I shook my head. I decided that coming to this reunion was a bad idea. I walked away and looked for my mom. Maybe we could go to that cool wax museum I'd heard about. At least wax people can't yell at you and make you feel bad.

"Attention! Attention please, for announcements!" I looked up and saw Dr. Mal, the head of the camp, standing with the microphone at the front of the room. Everybody started crowding into the area, pushing me forward into the room and farther from the exit. There was no getting out now.

"I would like to welcome you all to the sixth annual Camp Rituhbukkee reunion weekend," Dr. Mal said. "We started doing this so all those campers who became so close over the summer would have an opportunity to catch up with one another during the year. It's quickly become one of our most popular camp events."

I searched the crowd for my mom and saw her talking to Dr. Singer, who was one of the original founders of the camp. He was very distinguished-looking, which is how my mom taught me to describe people who are really, really old. He was also really nice! But mostly old.

Dr. Mal was saying, "We love gathering here at the New York Public Library, because it is one of the most glorious memorials to learning that we have in this country. Our campers have a special bond, which may well last a lifetime . . ."

My pocket buzzed. I snuck a look at my phone—a text from Jake. Okay, cool, I could use a little good news.

Hey Charlie Joe. Thanks for your text but I think it's best if we're not friends for a while. Maybe someday but not right now. Sorry.

I felt my face start to get red. I texted back.

Then why aren't you mad at Hannah? It takes two people to kiss, in case you haven't heard.

Two seconds later, Jake replied.

None of your business Charlie Joe. Please stay out of it before you cause any more problems.

All of a sudden I felt like if I didn't get out of there, I would explode.

I started pushing through the crowd again, this time in the opposite direction. I didn't know where I was headed, I just knew it had to be out of that room. I knocked into a few people, and once they saw it was me, they rolled their eyes. I'd kind of been the camp troublemaker, believe it or not.

"Hey, where ya goin'?" someone whispered. I turned and saw Jack Strong, wearing a Tufts University sweatshirt. Usually Jack wore only Ivy League shirts. I'd never heard of Tufts, which must have meant he was lowering his expectations a bit.

"Gotta get some air," I told him. Then I stopped. "You wanna come?"

Jack glanced up at Dr. Mal, then over at his parents, who were listening intently.

"Come on," I said. "Just for a minute. We'll come right back."

"What the heck." Jack slipped behind me, and we wound our way silently through the crowd. Once we got to the very back of the room, we took a quick left and headed down a long hall. We ducked into the first doorway we saw, which happened to be a huge room, where people were sitting at long tables, doing what looked like a superintense kind of homework.

Jack and I looked at each other.

"Nah," we said.

We left that room and headed back down the hall. There was a set of stairs on the left, with a red velvet rope across them.

KEEP OUT.

I stepped over the rope and headed down the stairs.

"Hey!" Jack said. "You're not supposed to go down there!"

But I didn't answer, and two seconds later, I heard him right behind me.

At the bottom of the stairs was a half-open door. We pushed it open to reveal another long hall, which was dimly lit—kind of like our unfinished basement back home. It felt like people hadn't really been down there in a long time.

"We should go back," Jack said, nervously.

I was a little nervous, too, but I'd also noticed something: The more nervous I got, the more I was able to put the whole Katie thing out of my mind.

"In a minute," I said, trying to sound cool.

As we walked slowly down the hall, things got a little creepier. There were some weird paintings on the wall of guys in long gray wigs. There was a half-eaten sandwich on the floor that looked like it might have been from 1932. And when I glanced up and saw a long spiderweb hanging down from one of the barely working lights, I realized there's only a certain amount of nervousness one person can take.

"Jack?"

"Yeah?" For some reason we were whispering, even though there wasn't a person in sight.

"Um, I think this is totally cool down here, but if you want to go back, we can."

"Okay."

We turned around and started heading back, when Jack stopped at a door.

RARE MANUSCRIPTS AND BOOKS: FIRST EDITIONS, AUTOGRAPHED. AUTHORIZED ENTRY ONLY.

"Whoa," Jack said. He was really into books, like everyone at Camp Rituhbukkee.

"Come on, we gotta go," I said, a little embarrassed that I'd become the scaredy-cat.

"Just a quick look," Jack said, pushing the door open. The room was even dimmer than the hallway, so we both took out our cellphones for light. There were books *everywhere*. Books, books, and more books. Did I mention *books*?

"People are going to start wondering where we are," I said. Hey, you can't blame a guy for trying.

Jack was going down a row of books. "Faulkner . . . Norman Mailer . . . Whitman . . ."

"Are those writers?" I asked. Jack looked at me like I was from Mars. Which, book-wise, I was.

"Mark Twain!" he exclaimed. A cold shiver ran through my body. Him, I knew—ever since my sixth birthday, when my dad gave me the entire Mark Twain collection for Christmas. Needless to say, that did not go well.

"That's it, I'm leaving," I said, heading out. But right by the door, there was a book lying on the floor that caught my eye.

I picked it up, dusted it off, and read the title: *Elizabethan Love Sonnets*.

Hmm.

I didn't know what *Elizabethan* or *Sonnets* meant, but I was familiar with "Love."

Way *too* familiar.

I picked up the book and started thumbing through it. The first thing I thought was, *I'm pretty sure this is*

English, but I can't understand a word of it. The second thing I thought was, *That just proves that love is totally un-understandable.*

And the third thing I thought was, *What was that?*

"What was that?" Jack asked, proving he was thinking the same thing I was. Then we heard it again. A noise.

We both froze in place and listened. Footsteps that sounded like they were coming from the stairs, and two voices that were getting closer. I could hear a few words here and there:

"Not sure how it got open . . ."

"Phil is getting the key . . ."

"Don't tell the boss . . ."

Then, the footsteps stopped. Jack and I looked at each other and waited, hoping the silence meant that the voices were gone.

They weren't.

Two seconds later, a third voice added: "You guys owe me." We heard a push . . . a squeak . . . and finally, a SLAM!

Jack and I waited another minute and then slowly made our way out of the rare book room and back down the hall toward the stairs. For some reason, though, we couldn't see the stairs. Then, the reason became clear.

The door that led to them had been shut.

Panic rose up in my throat, and I started running toward the door, Jack right behind me. We both knew before we got there that it had been locked tight. But we still tried to turn the giant door handle about a thousand times.

Eventually, we gave up. My heart was pounding.

"Charlie Joe?" Jack said, his voice shaking a little bit.

"Yeah?"

"Are you thinking what I'm thinking?"

"Probably not."

What he was probably thinking was, *We're trapped in the basement and we need to come up with a way to get out, or else our parents are going to kill us.*

What I was thinking was, *When you go into a giant building filled with books, bad things are bound to happen.*

Jack and I stared at each other, as we realized we were trapped in the basement of the New York Public Library. Then we did the only thing that made sense.

We screamed for help.

"HELP! ANYBODY! HELP! HELP!" We pounded on the door, too, over and over and over again.

After about fifty *helps*, we gave up.

"Okay, we need to figure out a way to get back upstairs," I said, checking my phone. No reception.

"D'uh," Jack answered. He was glaring at me, as if the whole thing were my fault.

"This whole thing is your fault," he snapped, confirming my suspicions.

"What are you talking about? How is it my fault?"

He snorted. "Because it was your idea to leave the reception, and it was your idea to go down the stairs."

Oh, that.

"Yeah, but you're the one who wanted to go in that stupid room full of old books," I reminded him.

"I don't want to talk to you right now," Jack said. "Unless you have an idea about how to get back upstairs."

That ended the conversation.

We walked back down the hall, passing the room with the rare books. There was another room on the left—the door said MAPS AND GEOGRAPHICAL ARTIFACTS. I poked my head in and saw a lot of books. A few feet farther down, there was a room on the right—the door said A HISTORY OF MEDICAL SCIENCE, VOLUMES 1–64. I poked my head in—books and more books. The next room was also on the right—BIBLIOGRAPHICAL RESEARCH, 1679–1729. I didn't even poke my head into that one.

All in all, it turned out to be the longest hallway in America, with about forty rooms, all of which were completely filled with shelves and shelves and shelves of books. There wasn't a single person in any of the rooms.

Finally, we turned a corner and saw a door that looked familiar.

"No way," I said.

"Way," Jack said.

It was the door that we'd come in through at the bottom of the stairs. Which meant we'd spent the last fifteen minutes going in a giant circle. Or, to be totally accurate, a giant square.

"I think we might be trapped for life," Jack said. He was kidding. Kind of.

All of a sudden I felt incredibly tired.

"You're right, by the way," I said, slumping down to sit on the floor. "This *is* all my fault."

"Oh, stop it," Jack said.

"No, it is." I paused for a second. "The thing is, I was really looking forward to coming to the reunion, because my life isn't going so great right now."

"Why not?"

"Because I'm an idiot, that's why." I found a quarter in my pocket and started scraping the floor with it. "A lot of my friends back home are mad at me."

"Well, it can't be the first time they're mad at you," Jack said, sitting down next to me. "I'm sure everyone will get over it. They always do."

"Not this time."

"Why? Did you do something terrible?"

I couldn't bring myself to go into the gory details. "It was basically all a stupid misunderstanding," I said. "I didn't mean to hurt anybody. But I think it might be too late to fix it."

Jack smacked me on the shoulder. "Charlie Joe, you're the one who told me at camp that you have to stand up for yourself. And when I got back home, I remembered what you said, and I went on strike to get my parents to let me quit some of my activities. And it worked! So now, I'm telling you the same thing: Don't give up. Figure out what's wrong, and fix it. If anyone can do it, you can."

I looked at Jack and nodded. Even though I'd talked him into leaving the reception with me, and dragged him downstairs just to get trapped in the basement, he was still a good enough friend to try and make me feel better.

Sometimes people can really surprise you, you know that?

"You're right," I said. "Once we get back to civilization, I'm gonna try and figure it out. Thanks for listening."

But Jack wasn't listening, at least not anymore. Instead, he was staring down the hall. "Hold on a second. What's that?"

"What?"

He pointed at a small door that we hadn't noticed before. The door said ELECTRICAL.

We looked at each other. "Electrical what?" I asked.

Jack shrugged. "Books, I guess."

But there was something about this room that felt different. I put my ear to the door and heard a loud hum coming from inside.

"Let's check it out." I opened the door and saw a long, flat machine sitting on a table, with a zillion wires poking out in every direction. On top of the machine sat five huge computers, stacked on top of each other, all blinking like crazy.

And, most important, there was a vent at the top of the room that was partially open.

Jack followed my gaze up to the vent and immediately said, "Hey, wait a second," but he was too late. I'd already started climbing up.

"Watch it!" Jack yelled, but the only thing I was watching was the vent, which was my ticket to freedom.

Jack swore under his breath, then started following me on the great computer climb.

When I reached the vent, Jack was just below me.

"Give me a push?" I asked.

"A push?"

"Yup. Shove me through."

Jack pushed my back, and I pushed my shoulder into the vent, trying to open it the rest of the way. After about five shoulder shoves, I'd gotten half my body through, but then got stuck, because the vent was actually pretty small. I gave one last push and launched myself off the last computer.

And all of a sudden I was through the vent!

The only problem was, as soon as I made it through the vent and onto the floor above me, all the lights went out.

"That's not good," Jack said.

"Ya think? I think I must have kicked one of the wires out or something. Can you take a look?"

I heard a sad laugh. "Uh, I would, but the lights are out."

I started groping in the dark, as I heard voices all around me saying, "What happened? Did the power go out? What was that?"

I looked down and could make out Jack with his cell phone, trying to put the wire back in.

"Any luck?" I whispered.

"I have no idea!" Jack said, not whispering at all. "I'm good at Math and Science, not Shop." But after a few more seconds and a little more fiddling, Jack somehow managed to figure it out, because the lights went back on. I immediately pulled him up through the vent, and he made it, too!

"We did it!" I yelled.

"I know!" he yelled back.

We lay on the ground, covered in grime and dust balls, laughing and high-fiving each other, enjoying our new-found freedom.

Until we noticed we were surrounded by feet.

Which was when we realized that we'd catapulted right back into the middle of the reception.

We looked up and saw everyone from Camp Rituhbuk-kee staring down at us. Two hundred people. And standing right in front of us was Dr. Mal.

I scrambled to my feet. "Hey, Dr. Mal," I said, offering him my filthy hand. "We were just . . . uh . . . having a look around the library."

Dr. Mal cocked his giant, bald head. "Charlie Joe Jackson," he said. "How I've missed you so."

I laughed awkwardly and looked around the room. The first person I saw was my mom, who didn't exactly look thrilled. Then I saw George and Nareem and the guys from the cabin, staring at me in shock. I saw Lauren Rubin, who had made it to the reunion after all.

And finally, I saw Katie, who was just staring at me, shaking her head.

I turned back to Dr. Mal, who still had the microphone in his hand. I asked him the first thing that popped into my head.

"Have you been talking this whole time?"

George Feedleman's
Guide to Romance

GIRLS ARE LIKE BOOKS. YOU NEED TO READ THEM CAREFULLY.

For a long time, I was the dumbest smart person in the world. Meaning, I was good at subjects like History and Geometry, but horrible at subjects like girls and dating. And the thing is, they don't teach you that stuff in school! But then, I realized that girls are like any other subject you don't know a lot about: The more you know, the more confident you get. Now, I'm not talking about studying girls like some weird scientist. I'm talking about just allowing yourself to discover things that make them easier to understand. Like, for instance, most girls do NOT want you to overcompliment them, because then they'll think you're a phony and that you don't mean any of it. But every once in a while, saying they look really nice or that their joke was really funny can make a girl's day. Stuff like that.

So, I guess what I'm saying is, it's good to be smart. But it's even better to be willing to learn.

After everything got sorted out, and Jack and I got cleaned up, and we managed to explain ourselves to the point where we knew we were not going to get thrown in jail, and I decided not to let the Katie thing ruin my night, the reception turned out to be really fun. The food was delicious, it was so great to see everyone again, and there was a DJ who actually played decent songs. (If you've ever been to a wedding, you know that's not always the case.) Before dessert, there was a slide show that showed a bunch of fun pictures from camp, like when we beat Wockajocka in basketball for the first time in twenty years (thanks to me, but I don't want to brag).

After the party, we all went back to the hotel, where George, Jack, and I convinced our parents to let us stay up for another hour. We decided to meet in George's room, because his parents said we could order ice cream sundaes from room service.

"What do you guys want to do?" I asked. "Wanna watch TV?"

George shrugged. "I don't watch TV."

Jack and I looked at George, then at each other. We shook our heads sadly.

"What?" George said. "I never get to see you guys. Let's just hang out and talk."

You know something? He had a good point.

So we talked about everything—school, parents, friends, movies, sports—but avoided the one topic that we all knew was the most important one of all. I'm not sure *why* we avoided it—probably because they were waiting for me to bring it up, and I didn't want to.

Finally, George couldn't take it anymore.

"I thought maybe, uh, we could, uh, you know, talk about . . ."

"Talk about what?" Jack asked.

George took a deep breath. "Girls."

There it was.

"I'm not sure there's that much to talk about," I said.

"I'm still going out with Cathy," George said, totally ignoring me. "We've seen each other twice since the summer. She's awesome, but I'm not sure what to do. I like this other girl at school, and there are these two other girls who like me."

So George was the superstud among us. I needed a minute to let that sink in.

He punched Jack in the shoulder. "And how about you? After that whole thing you pulled with going on strike to protest your parents overscheduling you, and refusing to get off your couch, and going on TV and everything, I bet the girls must be all over you!"

"Kind of," Jack admitted.

I stared at my two camp friends. One was tall and dorky with a slight skin condition, and the other was quiet and shy and wore nothing but college logo shirts. And they had girls coming out of the woodwork! If I told them the truth about me, I'd be the laughingstock of the reunion. I'd be the camp joke. I'd be—

"I've never actually had a girlfriend," I heard myself blurt out.

You know something? It was a relief to be able to tell them.

George and Jack looked at each other.

"Seriously?" George said.

"But you're the man," Jack said.

"And at camp, you gave me tips about kissing," George said.

"And you're so funny and confident," Jack said.

"And you—"

"Yes, seriously," I said. "Never. Never ever ever."

I let that bomb do its damage for a second, then I added, "And all my friends have one."

No one talked for a minute.

"Oh," George said, finally.

But I still wasn't finished. "And it's not just that. It's worse. I'm having major girl problems. It took me a while but I finally admitted to myself that Katie was the girl I really liked all along. But then, she saw me kissing this other girl that I used to totally like, and now Katie hates me and won't even talk to me, and I don't know what to do because I've never really felt like this before and it feels totally horrible."

For a minute, the only sound in the room was George scraping the bottom of his sundae bowl with his spoon.

"Oh, now I get it," Jack said, nodding his head sadly.

"What about Zoe Alvarez?" George asked. Ah, Zoe. She was the girl I'd talked about at camp, since we kind of liked each other before the summer.

"Zoe moved, and I was going to go visit her, but I didn't have any money, so I tried to raise some money by having a fake bar mitzvah, but I ended up almost destroying my house and getting grounded for about half a century," I said. That put an end to all discussion about Zoe Alvarez.

George got us three sodas out of the little refrigerator in his room.

"Don't we have to pay for these?" Jack asked.

"Nah, it's all included," George said. I guess he wasn't a genius about everything.

Jack took a big swig. "So what are you going to do about the Katie thing?"

Just then there was a knock on the door. Jack suddenly looked panicked, like it was the soda police coming to arrest him for stealing.

"Who could that be?" he asked.

George and I shrugged.

When George got up to open the door, Nareem was standing there. Nareem, as in Katie's ex-boyfriend.

My heart jumped up into my mouth.

"Hey," Nareem said. "Jack's mom told my mom you guys were here."

"I thought you went out to dinner," I said.

"We just got back." Nareem came over and sat down on the couch. I tried to smile, but inside I was wondering how I could change the subject to something Nareem liked talking about. Quantum physics, maybe—

"Charlie Joe was just telling us that he likes Katie, but she doesn't like him," George announced.

"Hold on a second," I said, but it was too late. Nareem was staring at me. If you looked closely, you could see his head barely nodding up and down.

"I'm glad to hear you finally admit it," he said, his voice just above a whisper. "Even if it was George who actually said it."

"Oh, dang it," George said. He was finally realizing that this might be a sensitive subject for Nareem, considering that Katie had broken up with him a few months earlier. Definitely scratch that whole George-is-a-genius thing.

"Yeah," I said. Which I think was an answer to both George and Nareem. "I'm—I'm sorry about that, Nareem."

Nareem got up and stared out the window, at the lit-up city. "Have you said anything to Katie? Have you been very clear with her? Instead of avoiding it, like you have been doing practically since I've known you?"

"What do you mean by that?" I asked.

"It was very obvious to me that you liked Katie!" Nareem said. He wasn't whispering anymore, not by a long shot.

George coughed nervously. "Hey, does anyone want to order cheesecake?" he asked. "My mom said it would be cool if we wanted to order cheesecake." He waited for someone to answer him, but no one did. "Or not."

"You're right," I said to Nareem. "I think I liked Katie longer than I realized. I don't know, we were just regular friends for so long, and I had this crush on Hannah Spivero for like forever. Then suddenly it seemed like everything changed, and I didn't know how to deal with it. Especially since you were kind of going out with her at the time."

"That's true, I was," Nareem said, his voice soft again as he remembered.

"Um, I have a crazy idea," Jack said.

We all looked at him.

"Why don't you just tell her the truth?"

George nodded his head in agreement.

"I've been trying!" I said. "It's not that easy!"

Nareem took off his glasses and started cleaning them with his shirt. I think he just needed something to do. "Love is never easy," he said. "It is hard work. Which is also what makes it so rewarding."

Sometimes it was hard to believe he was only in middle school.

"You should tell her before we all leave tomorrow morning," George said to me. "That way, we can be there for moral support."

"You should," Jack said.

"Indeed you should," Nareem said.

I stared at my three friends, knowing they were right. Ugh! Couldn't I just stay up here in George's room forever, where it was safe and we had ice cream and satellite television, and there was no danger of rejection?

Love is never easy.

"Let's order that cheesecake," I said.

Sunday morning breakfast was everyone's last chance to hang around together before heading back home, so it was completely mobbed by the time I made it downstairs to the restaurant. I saw Katie in the distance, out of the corner of my eye, sitting at a table with a bunch of our friends. I started to walk over, but then I had a better idea.

The better idea involved doing anything else.

I went up to the buffet and got some eggs, poured myself a glass of juice, and started looking for a place to sit. The first person I saw was Ms. Domerca.

"Charlie Joe!" she exclaimed. "Come eat with us!"

It wasn't until I sat down that I realized she was sitting with Dr. Mal and a bunch of adults and kids I'd never seen before.

Dr. Mal didn't look all that thrilled to see me, to be honest.

"Good morning, Mr. Jackson," he said.

"Morning, Dr. Mal," I said back.

"Charlie Joe," Ms. D. said, "this is perfect timing. I'm not sure if you know this, but we also use these reunion breakfasts to meet with families who are not yet part of the Camp Rituhbukkee community, so that we might give them a sense of who we are and what we're about."

I introduced myself to the three kids. They smiled awkwardly. Nerds-in-training, for sure.

"Perhaps you can tell them what Rituhbukkee is like, from a camper's perspective," Ms. Domerca continued.

Dr. Mal made a face like he'd just eaten a rotten egg.

"Well," I said, "let me just start by saying, Camp Rituhbukkee is not for everyone."

Dr. Mal made a face like the rotten egg had just laid new rotten eggs inside his stomach.

"It's not for kids who aren't interested in the world," I continued. "Or kids who don't want to improve themselves. Or kids who don't want to be around other kids that are so curious, and so interesting, that it will make them push themselves to be more curious and more interesting themselves." I smiled brightly at the adults, since they were the ones who were going to be writing the checks. "Like I said, this camp is not for everyone. Which is what makes it the best camp in the world."

"Well, that's very impressive," said one of the parents, a guy who seemed like one of those Dads who wouldn't be satisfied unless his kid grew up to be president of the United States.

Dr. Mal let out a big, relieved breath, while Ms. Domerca looked at me like, *I knew you could do it.*

I looked across the restaurant and saw George waving

at me, like, *Stop stalling!* Then Jack saw me, and he started waving me over, too.

"Well I'm going to go join my friends," I said to the table. "They're the greatest group of guys in the world, and the fact that I'm not going to see them again until the summer fills me with great sorrow and regret."

"That'll do, Charlie Joe," Dr. Mal said, that rotten-egg look flashing across his face for a quick second.

"Right." I got up and headed over to my friends' table. Everyone was in the middle of a loud conversation, which immediately stopped as soon as they saw me coming.

"Hey, you guys," I said. I shuffled my feet, while everyone waited for me to sit down. "Um, Katie? Could I talk to you for a second?"

She was taking a sip of juice, which turned out to be the longest sip of juice ever recorded. Finally, she put the glass down. "Sure."

I pointed at a bench in the corner of the room. "Could we maybe . . . go over there?"

"Sure," she said again.

I put my tray down on the table, and we walked over to the bench. I sat down. Katie didn't.

"Are you going to sit down?" I asked her.

She barely rolled her eyes—just enough so I could see it—then sat down.

"What's up." She said it less like a question and more like a demand.

"I just thought we should talk."

"Can't we talk at home? We don't have a lot of time left with the camp kids."

"I want to talk now."

"Fine."

Then she looked at me, finally, directly, intensely, for the first time since she saw me kiss Hannah.

And she waited.

And I thought of everything I'd wanted to say for the last five days . . . everything I felt . . . every truth I wanted to tell her . . . and I froze.

"Um . . ."

She kept staring. And I kept saying nothing.

"Uh-oh, my bad," I finally said. "I gotta go to the bathroom."

And I ran out of the restaurant.

I could feel the sweat trickling down my back and I dashed into the men's room, to get myself together. I was so frustrated, I threw my backpack down in anger, and the whole thing spilled open.

"ARRGHH!" I screamed.

I bent down to pick everything up, when something caught my eye. A book cover. It looked strange, but familiar. I picked it up.

Elizabethan Love Sonnets. I couldn't believe it! How did that get in there? I thought for a second and realized that when I was in the library basement and we heard voices, I must have panicked and shoved the book in my backpack. Then I forgot all about it.

Oh, man! I was sunk. I was history. I was done for. I was—

Wait a second.

I was saved.

I grabbed the book and opened it. Then I took out my notebook and started writing as fast as I could.

Approximately seven minutes later,
I ran back into the restaurant, where Katie was back sitting with the gang.

"Katie!" I said, apparently at a volume loud enough for many more people other than Katie to hear.

She looked at me. She was clearly getting fed up, but she was too nice a person to come out and say it. So instead she just said, "Yes?"

"I wrote you a poem," I announced. "Sometimes it's hard for me to say what I mean, so I wrote it down."

This actually got her to smile at me, for the first time in what seemed like a year. "You wrote me a poem?"

"Yup! I've been reading a lot of poetry lately and I thought I'd give it a try. Can I read it to you?"

A quick look of distrust crossed her face—probably because of the reading comment—but she decided to give me the benefit of the doubt. "Sure, I'd like that."

I took a deep breath, got out my notebook, and started reading.

"I would compare you to a summer's day
Although, now that I think about it, you're
   even more temperate, I'd say!
And May, darling, is when the rough winds
   blew
And summer is almost as hot as you—"

"Wait, Charlie Joe," said Lauren Rubin, interrupting. "You're kidding, right?"

I looked up. "What do you mean, kidding?" I glanced at Katie, who had her head down, and I felt a drop of sweat on my forehead as I heard the other kids giggle. Uh-oh. This wasn't going to end well.

"Well, um, I hate to tell you," Lauren said, "but you didn't exactly write that."

"I didn't?"

"Nope. Shakespeare did."

My eyes bugged out of my head a little bit. "Shakespeare? No way."

Katie looked up, with pity in her eyes. "Way," she said.

"How would you guys know that?" I said, panic starting to rise in my throat. "That's crazy!"

"That's like one of the most famous poems ever written," Katie said, almost apologetically. "You just changed it a little."

"Yeah, like, made it horrible," snorted some girl I didn't know. I made a mental note to keep not knowing her my whole life.

Another girl held up her phone. "I found the real poem," she announced. Then she started reading.

> *"Shall I compare thee to a summer's day*
> *Thou art more lovely and more temperate*
> *Rough winds to shake the darling buds of*
> *   May—"*

"Okay, okay!" I shouted. "Stop! I get it!" I hung my head. "I found it in a book called *Elizabethan Love Sonnets*. So, uh, I thought it was, you know, written by someone named Elizabeth."

A few kids giggled at that one. Eric Cunkler raised his hand like he was in class. "'Elizabethan' means the period when Elizabeth the First was queen," he said.

I felt a little nauseous. Why did everyone at Camp Rituhbukkee have to be so freakin' *smart*?

"Charlie Joe, I don't get it," Katie said, getting up. "Don't you remember at camp, when Jared wanted to cheat off of Lauren, and you helped put a stop to it? This is kind of the same thing."

I don't know what kind of face I was making right then, but it must have been a pretty pathetic one, because she actually put her hand on my shoulder in a comforting way. "You're such a smart person, Charlie Joe, but you do the craziest things sometimes. As if I would ever believe that you would write a poem like that. Jeez Louise."

She had a good point. I had no idea what *temperate* even meant.

As Katie sat back down, she looked up at me one last time.

"See you at home," she said. And then she added, so softly that only I could hear it, "Thanks for trying."

I stood there for about another minute, watching all the kids whispering and giggling. The only person who didn't seem to think it was hilarious was Nareem. He just kind of smiled at me, with a sad look in his eyes.

Finally I ran out of there, with one thought running through my mind.

Love can make you really, really dumb.

"You left without saying goodbye to anyone," George said.

"Yeah, what was that about?" Jack said.

It was fifteen minutes later, and we were all in the hotel lobby, waiting for our parents to check out.

"Nothing," I said, avoiding eye contact.

"Well, see you next summer," Jack said.

"Have a great rest of the year," George added.

"You guys, too." And that was about it. There wasn't much more to add. "I should go."

I turned to go find my mom.

George held out his hand to stop me. "Charlie Joe, wait."

I stopped.

"Katie likes you," Jack said. "I can tell. She really likes you."

"Or, she *would* like you," George added, "if you didn't keep trying so hard to mess it up."

I shook my head. "Thanks you guys, but you're wrong. She used to, maybe, but not anymore."

"*You're* the one who's wrong, Charlie Joe," Jack said. "You just need to be yourself."

George laughed a little. "You know, your usual obnoxious, annoying self."

"Just be myself," I said. "That's funny. I read that in a book once."

Jack and George stared at me.

"No, seriously," I said. "I did. And I tried it. But it turned out, myself told me to say that liking her would be gross, like liking my sister. And myself told me to copy a poem out of a book that I thought no one would have heard of, but which turned out to be the most famous poem ever written."

"Well technically, that's not being yourself," George said. "That's being someone else."

"D'uh," Jack added, for emphasis.

George sat down on a bench, and we sat down next to him. "What you need is to do something really special and romantic and stuff, but that's from your heart—not from some book."

"Hey wait a second," I said. "Wasn't I giving you girl advice last summer?"

"Times change," George answered.

I thought for a minute. What could I possibly do that was special and romantic? I was in middle school, for crying out loud. I was just trying to get my homework done with a minimum of effort.

Which gave me an idea.

"Hey, I have to do a class project on someone I consider

a personal hero," I told the guys. "It's due in like a week. I was going to do it on my dad, but maybe I'll do it on Katie instead! What do you guys think?"

George and Jack looked at each other, then back at me.

"You're kidding, right?" Jack said.

"That's the exact opposite of what I'm talking about," George said. "That's just like sucking up to her."

Jack put his hand on my shoulder as if I were five years old. "It's better if you do something that won't embarrass her to the point where she never speaks to you again."

Okay, so scratch that.

George scrunched up his eyes, which meant he was about to say something very intelligent. My friend Jake Katz does the same thing. I think it's in the Genius Handbook. "Maybe you can do some research and find a hero that you actually think would be an awesome choice, but who's interesting and different enough that Katie would think it was cool, too," he said. "Or someone Katie already thinks is awesome. At least that would give you guys something to talk about, and who knows what would happen after that."

"That sounds impossible," I said. "Plus, it sounds like it would involve a lot of research. I like my projects to have as little research as possible."

They sighed and shook their heads. Then George got out his phone and started recording me. "Can you say that again? The part about doing as little research as possible? I told the guys back home about my camp friend whose goal in life was to make it through middle school without ever reading a book, but they didn't believe me. I need some actual evidence."

I made a face into the camera. "Yo yo yo, this is Charlie Joe Jackson, big fan of not reading. The only book I like is my grandma's checkbook, you know what I'm sayin'?"

The guys laughed. "See?" Jack said. "You're actually kind of funny when you're just being normal."

"Good luck with your assignment without doing any reading," George said, still recording me.

"Yeah, whatever," I said. George was right, though. As if there were some way that I could do a report about someone Katie really cares about, without reading. That sounded ridiculous. That sounded completely impossible. That sounded—

Wait a second.

I smacked George on the back. "You're a genius."

"I've heard," he said. Then he added, "Ow."

"I have an idea," I said.

"Is it a crazy idea?" Jack asked.

"I think so."

George whistled. "Remember what happened the last time you had a crazy idea?"

"It was about fifteen minutes ago," Jack chimed in.

"You two are quite the comedy team," I said.

I picked up my backpack, ready to get back to the real world. So what if my last crazy idea hadn't worked out? I couldn't worry about that. I had to look ahead. I had to have faith.

I had to give it one last shot.

I hugged Jack and George goodbye. Then I left the hotel, the city, the crowded streets, the building filled with books, the scary basements, and the most embarrassing moment of my life behind.

Claire Jackson's
Guide to Romance

PATIENCE. PATIENCE. PATIENCE.

My husband drives me crazy. He never puts his clothes away, he lets the dogs on every bed and couch in the house, and I'm not sure if he even knows how to use the washer and dryer. But guess what? I drive him crazy, too. I never answer my cell phone, I'm always late, and I've been known to lock myself out of the car.

Despite all that, though, we love each other. A lot. And even though we make each other nuts sometimes, that's part of the deal.

So here's my advice: Don't get scared off by someone you like, just because they might have some habits that annoy you a little. Learn to be patient. It's part of learning how to love.

But just between you and me . . . why can't men ever pick up their socks?!?!?!

As soon as I got home, I started videoing everything my family did.

I filmed the dogs sleeping and playing outside.

They were cool with it.

Then I filmed my mom paying bills.

"What are you doing?" she asked.

"Filming you paying bills."

"Why?"

"It's for a school project," I explained.

"Aha," she said, clearly suspicious. But she let me keep filming.

I filmed my sister twirling her hair while she was on the phone in the front yard.

"Cut it out!" she yelled.

"It's for a school project!"

"I don't care! I don't have any makeup on!"

I kept filming until she threw her sandal at me.

I filmed my dad when he came home from work. My dad is almost always singing when he walks in the door. I guess that's because he's in a good mood, which is probably because he's home from work, which makes a lot of sense to me.

Anyway, that night, after he walked in the door and dropped his briefcase on the floor, he saw me pointing my phone at him and stopped singing.

"Charlie Joe, what are you doing?"

"Filming."

"Filming what?"

"The family."

"Why?"

"School project."

I followed him up the stairs until he turned around.

"Don't school projects usually involve reading and writing?"

I hesitated.

I wasn't sure I wanted to tell him that my paper on my personal hero wasn't going to be an actual paper at all.

That I'd figured out a way to do a great job without having to do any actual reading and writing.

So instead I just said, "Don't worry. I have to get a good grade on this project or else for the rest of the year I have to spend recess in Mrs. Sleep's office."

That seemed to satisfy my dad. "Okay, fine," he said. "Just don't film me putting on my pajamas."

I put down my phone—the battery was about to run out anyway.

"What's the assignment?" my dad asked.

"Um . . . it's complicated."

He squinted at me. "Complicated how?"

I tried to figure out how to answer him. I didn't want to tell anyone what the actual assignment was, because then they would have acted differently. I wanted everything to be normal. I wanted people to see that my hero was great, just because of how he acted, every day.

"It's a secret," I admitted, finally.

My dad shook his head, but then he put on his slippers and sighed happily, and I knew everything would be okay. I'd heard him say many times that putting on his slippers was a highlight of his day.

"A secret," he said. "Well, it better be an A-plus secret."

"Oh, it is, Dad, I promise."

So I filmed at dinner.

I filmed after dinner, while we watched TV.

I filmed when we took the dogs for a walk.

When I filmed my sister, Megan, eating ice cream, she said, "Just make sure I don't look fat." Two seconds later, she said, "Turn that thing off."

"But you don't look fat!" I said.

She shook her head. "Eating ice cream makes anyone look fat."

I turned the camera off.

Then I turned it back on two seconds later.

As the week went on, I didn't tell anyone about my project—not my family, not my friends at school, not my teacher. I just kept shooting. I started editing over the weekend, since the assignment was due on Monday. I got it down to the best three minutes, but I realized something was missing. Everything I'd filmed was in the house or the yard. I felt like the video had to end with a family trip of some kind, so I convinced everyone to go to Lake Monahan. It's an awesome place, even though it was where I started my unfortunate dog-walking business, which ended up involving a missing dachshund, a playful Great Dane, and a very lucky gopher that cheated death.

Anyway, on Sunday morning we all piled in the car—dogs included, of course—and headed out to the lake. It was a pretty cloudy day, so there weren't as many people as there usually were. But Moose and Coco didn't care. They made a beeline into the water, as Megan, my parents, and I set up a delicious lunch at the picnic table. Well, to be fair, *they* set up the lunch. I was busy shooting.

"Is this documentary thingie just your latest way of getting out of doing any chores?" Megan asked me.

I kept filming. "Hopefully."

"I don't get it, Charlie Joe," my dad said. "You're video-taping us doing boring stuff like watching TV and eating lunch. Doesn't seem very exciting."

"Yeah," my mom added, "how come you don't want us to jump out of an airplane or something?"

"Have you ever jumped out of an airplane?" I asked her.

"Uh, that'd be a no."

"That's why."

"Hey, check it out," Megan said, pointing a few picnic tables down. "Who's that kid with all your girlfriends?"

I stood up to take a look. The first thing I saw was Hannah Spivero's dog, Gladys, wagging her tail. Then I saw what she was wagging at: Hannah, Eliza, and Katie, who were laughing hysterically at something Emory, the new kid from California, had just said.

"Huh," I said.

"Well, aren't you going to go say hi?" asked my mom. "At least tell them to come over here. I never got a chance to say goodbye to Katie in the city."

"But we're in the middle of lunch," I said.

My dad looked up from his plate just long enough to say, "Don't be rude."

I sighed, put down my phone, and walked over to their table. They didn't see me coming until I was about two feet away. Then Eliza smiled, got up, and gave me a big hug. (Ever since she'd stopped liking me and started liking

127

Emory, she'd been a lot nicer to me. That's how girls work.)

"Charlie Joe, what are you doing here?"

"Hanging with the family."

Emory got up and gave me some California version of a handshake that was pretty complicated, but I tried to keep up.

"Hey, dude," he said.

Hannah came over and gave me a hug, too. Things were okay between us, considering the kiss and everything. Jake and her were totally back to being a normal couple. I guess they talked about everything and worked it out like two mature people.

I should try that sometime.

That left Katie. I looked at her. "Hey."

"Hey."

We all stood there, not saying anything, for a few too many seconds.

"So what are you guys doing here?" I asked.

"Dude, we're celebrating finishing our Personal Hero projects," Emory said. "It's the sweetest feeling in the world, dude." I was starting to think Emory was worried he would get arrested if he didn't use the word *dude* in every sentence.

"Cool," I said. Then I looked around.

"Jake is still working on his," Hannah said, answering my question before I could ask it.

"Cool," I said again. "Well, I better get back."

"What about your paper, Charlie Joe?" Katie asked. "Are you done with it?"

I hesitated. It was nice that she was making an effort to have a conversation, but I was pretty sure I wouldn't like where the conversation ended up. Looking back on it, I could have just said "Fine," but for some reason I didn't.

"Well, uh, actually, I'm not writing a paper."

Katie's smile faded. "What do you mean, you're not writing a paper?"

"I mean, I'm not writing a paper. I decided to do something different."

"Can you do that?" Emory asked.

Katie stood up suddenly. "Charlie Joe, how long do you expect to get away with just doing whatever you want? Life doesn't work that way! Sometimes you have to play by the rules! The assignment was to write a paper, but for some reason you can't even do that. You can't keep treating everything like a joke! And you can't treat people like a joke, either! You need to grow up!"

No one moved for a minute.

"Are you saying I treat you like a joke?" I asked. "Because I don't."

Katie gave an exaggerated shrug of her shoulders. "Whatever. Do what you want, it's none of my business. I really don't care. Seriously."

"Okay," I answered. "Glad to know you don't care."

We stared at each other for a few seconds.

"You know something, Charlie Joe?" Katie said, finally. "You make me act mean. And you make me act petty, and you make me not like myself sometimes. Thanks for that. Thanks a lot."

And with that, she walked off toward the lake. I stood there for another minute, then I bent down to pet Gladys, who actually seemed happy to see me.

I went back to my family and sat down. That night, as I edited my school project on the computer, I thought about what Katie had said.

Sometimes you have to play by the rules.

She was right. Sometimes you do.

But not always.

"Hey, Mom?"

"What, honey?"

"I have a favor to ask you."

It was the next morning, and I was eating my favorite cereal, ChocoFrostees. My mom had tried to get me to stop eating sugary cereals for years, but eventually we compromised when I agreed to add in a banana, which actually made it taste even better (I didn't tell her that part).

"What's the favor?"

"I need you to come to school today."

"To pick you up?"

"No, during school."

She looked up from her computer. "How come?"

"Because I need you to bring me something."

"Okay, honey. What is it? Won't it fit in your backpack?"

"Nope," I said. "It's bigger than that. A lot bigger."

My mom sat down next to me. "Oooh, this sounds intriguing," she said. "Tell me everything."

So I did.

Pete Milano's hero was Angus Young, the guitarist for the band AC/DC. According to Pete, Angus "changed the face of music forever, and he changed it really loud."

"Thank you, Pete," said Ms. Albone. "Food for thought."

Pete looked confused. "What does food have to do with it?"

Betsy Armstrong's hero was Betsy Ross. We all just assumed it was because they had the same first name, but Betsy said it was because "She sewed the fabric of our nation."

"She most certainly did," said Ms. Albone. "Well done, Betsy."

Then it was Emory's turn. His hero was some surfer whose name I forget. I remember how many times Emory used the word *dude* in his paper, though. Forty-two.

"And for our final presentation of the day," Ms. Albone announced, Charlie Joe Jackson will tell us all about his personal hero."

Right at that moment, I noticed Mrs. Sleep slip into the classroom. Yikes, the pressure was really on now.

I went up to the front of the room. I could feel Katie's eyes on me. "Actually, Ms. Albone, I'm not."

"You're not?" asked Ms. Albone.

I walked behind her desk, reached up, and pulled the screen down. "I'm going to be doing something a little different."

"I see," Ms. Albone said. She looked skeptical for a second, but then she sat down.

I signaled to Jake, who turned the lights off. Then I plugged my computer into the projector in the back of the room. "Please enjoy this short film on my personal hero."

NARRATION:
Hello, my name is Charlie Joe Jackson, and I'd like to tell you a little bit about my personal hero.

A SHOT OF MY FAMILY EATING DINNER.
He is a member of my family.

A SHOT OF MY FAMILY WATCHING TV
And he is an incredibly important part of my life.

A SHOT OF MY FAMILY HANGING
OUT IN THE YARD
*I would even go so far as to
say he is one of my heroes.*

CLOSE-UP ON MOOSE, LYING IN
THE YARD.
My hero is my dog, Moose.

SHOTS OF MOOSE EATING,
SLEEPING, WAGGING HIS TAIL,
JUMPING IN THE LAKE, PLAYING
WITH COCO
*Moose is my hero because he
has the purest heart of
anyone I know.*

SHOT OF MOOSE ON THE COUCH,
RESTING HIS HEAD ON MEGAN'S
LAP
He is full of love.

SHOT OF MOOSE WAITING
PATIENTLY FOR FOOD AT DINNER
TABLE
And hope.

SHOT OF MOOSE GREETING DAD
AFTER COMING HOME FROM WORK
*He is always there when you
need him.*

SHOT OF MOOSE NUDGING MOM'S
ARM WHEN SHE'S TRYING TO TALK
ON THE PHONE
And even when you don't.

SHOT OF MOOSE GETTING UP FROM
HIS BED
*Moose has been a member of
our family for as long as I
can remember.*

SHOT OF MOOSE RUNNING OUTSIDE
*I used to think he would live
forever.*

SHOTS OF MOOSE WALKING,
RUNNING, AND LYING DOWN
*But then I realized he
wouldn't. I realized dogs live
a lot shorter lives than
people do. At first that made*

me really sad. But then it
made me more determined than
ever to make the most of our
time left together.

SELFIE SHOTS OF MOOSE AND ME,
PLAYING, HUGGING, EATING, JUST
GENERALLY HAVING AN AWESOME
TIME
I love you, Moose. And I
think you're a hero.

THE END

* * *

At the end of the movie, I turned the lights back on. Then I opened the door to the classroom, and my mom came in.

She had Moose with her.

The whole class went "AWWWWW."

I took the leash from my mom and walked Moose to the front of the classroom.

"Sit," I said.

Moose sat.

"This is Moose," I announced to the class. "I thought you guys might want to meet him. Some of you know him

already, but a lot of you don't. Moose is a chocolate Lab, and he's ten years old, which is getting pretty old for a Lab. But he can still do a lot of things a younger dog does." I held up a treat, and he jumped up to eat it. "But he is also definitely acting older—he doesn't run the way he used to, or go up the stairs as much. He doesn't jump on my bed anymore either, do you, you lazy beast." I gave Moose a rub. "I love Coco, too, my other dog, but Moose is older, so I've known him longer." I paused for a second. "I just wanted to make sure he knew that I thought he was great before he . . ." I looked at Moose, who was looking back at me like I was the only person in the world. "Before it was too late." I hugged

Moose, who gave me a big smooch. Then he turned around and gave Ms. Albone a smooch, too! Luckily, she laughed.

"Thank you," I said. "That is the end of my presentation."

I thanked my mom, who hugged me. "I'm so proud of you," she whispered.

I looked around the class. They were all quiet.

But it was the good kind of quiet.

I looked at Katie. She looked back at me.

"Charlie Joe," Ms. Albone said. She looked stern.

I waited nervously.

"That was not the assignment. The assignment was to write a research paper."

Uh-oh.

"I'm sorry, Ms. Albone."

Her face softened. "But, I am impressed with your creativity and sensitivity."

Phew.

Ms. Albone turned to the class. "Charlie Joe has made a strong statement on the gift of love and offered powerful testimony to the passage of time," she said. "He has shown us how it's the little things that make us great. And by us, I mean all living things, who are all equally precious." She turned back to me and shook my hand. "Congratulations. Well done."

"Thank you," I said.

I looked up and saw Mrs. Sleep in the back of the room.

She nodded at me, then left. It was an important nod. I was pretty sure it meant I could spend recess with my friends for the rest of the year.

The bell rang for the end of class. I hugged my mom and Moose goodbye, and Ms. Albone walked with them down to the office. As the other kids hurried out, most of them slapped me on the back, saying things like "That was awesome," "Great job," "Wow, that was intense," and other things like that.

It was a pretty cool feeling, I have to admit.

When everyone had gone, I went back to get my stuff.

Which was when I noticed Katie standing by my desk.

"Charlie Joe," she said.

"Yeah?"

"That was amazing."

I may have blushed. Okay, fine, I definitely did. "Thanks. I kind of . . . I knew that you would like it. I know how much you love Moose."

Katie seemed a little nervous. "I . . . I think I owe you an apology."

"No—" I began, but she cut me off.

"I do. I pretended not to care about the Hannah thing. I tried to just laugh it off. But I think the more I pretended, the more upset I became. And I started treating you badly. And I'm sorry."

"I have way more to be sorry for," I said. "Like . . . the kiss."

"You don't have to apologize for that," Katie said. "Not to me, anyway."

"Well, I'm really, really sorry I lied about writing that poem. That might have been the dumbest thing I've ever done."

Katie nodded. "At least that was dumb in a sweet way."

"Well, it's the last dumb thing I'm going to do for a long time. Like you said, Katie, it's time to grow up, and I'm gonna. I swear."

Katie smiled—a real smile. "Well, it seems like you've already started. And that's awesome."

We just stood there, not saying anything. I think we were both so relieved there wasn't this weird tension between us anymore that we wanted to enjoy it for a minute.

"And," I said, "all that stuff I said, about how liking you would be like liking my sister, and how it would be gross . . . that's why I did that poem thing, because I couldn't figure out how to tell you the truth."

Katie's eyes shined like really bright stars. "Which is what?"

"Which is—"

Suddenly the classroom door burst open.

"WHAT are you kids still doing in here?!" It was Mr. Margolis, the assistant principal. I think his entire job was to get kids in trouble, and he was really good at it. "I was walking by and I heard voices. Children's voices! Which didn't make sense, because I KNEW that EVERY student in this school should be in their assigned classrooms, and there's no class in this room during this period." Mr. Margolis walked toward us, twirling a pen in his hand. "But sure enough, the voices were REAL! Here you are! I'm sure there's a perfectly good reason for you to both be late for class, and I'd like to hear it."

Katie and I looked at each other.

"Well?" Mr. Margolis demanded. "Would you mind explaining to me what you're both doing in here?"

Katie smiled at me, picked up her backpack, and looked Mr. Margolis in the eye.

"Making up," she said.

Pete Milano's
Guide to Romance

BE ANNOYING!

So you'll probably read other people's advice on how it's important to be all nice and kind and the sweetest person ever to the person you like.

Don't believe it.

Because I have a secret: Girls like it when you totally get on their nerves.

No, I'm serious! They do. They might say they don't, they might tell you to get away from them or leave them alone, but secretly, they think it's fun. Girls like arguing. And if you act kind of like an idiot sometimes, they have a lot to argue about.

Nice guys finish last. Annoying guys finish with a girlfriend.

Part Three
FRIENDSHIP IS THE BEST SHIP

Sometimes, the best way to stand out is to fit in.

* * *

All children want to be noticed: It is a very natural behavior. And the temptation to show off in front of one's peers is also something most children are faced with. But part of the maturation process means resisting that temptation. It is not attractive to be the center of attention all the time. In fact, it often has the opposite effect: People start to resent those who demand to be noticed.

Think of it as a collection of people all trying to breathe the same air. If one person demands too much of that air, the other people will begin to suffer. And then they will turn against the one who is taking more than his fair share.

Remember: It is important to leave plenty of air for everyone else.

So that ended up being the closest I came to telling Katie I liked her for a while.

For the next month or so, nothing all that exciting happened. Katie and I were friends again—but not best friends, or boyfriend and girlfriend friends. Kind of weird, in-between friends.

And once people started figuring out that Katie and I maybe liked each other, things got even more awkward. Like sometimes at lunch, if Katie was sitting next to someone and I came up to the table with my tray, that person would get up, so I could sit next to Katie.

"You don't have to get up," I'd say.

"No, I want to," they'd answer.

So I'd sit down next to Katie, and we'd look at each other and talk about something totally meaningless.

"English homework was really hard last night," I'd say.

"You're not kidding," Katie'd say.

"That tuna sandwich you're eating looks good."

"It is."

Being in-between friends with a girl is not easy, let me tell you.

At least one part of my life got a lot less awkward,

though. It happened one day while I was standing in line for lunch.

Jake Katz was standing there, ignoring me as usual. Then, totally out of the blue, he said, "The French fries look particularly soggy today."

After looking around, I realized he was talking to me. I was shocked. It was the first time he'd started a conversation with me in six weeks.

"Huh?" I said.

"The French fries look soggy," he repeated.

It took me a minute to realize what was happening. He may have said, *The French fries look soggy*, but what he actually meant was, *I was really, really mad that you kissed my girlfriend, but a lot of time has passed, and I'm not that mad anymore, and I'm ready to be friends again.*

"Yeah," I said. "They are soggy. I'm going to have to talk to management about that."

And what *I* actually meant was, *Like I told you before, I'm really sorry that happened, it was a terrible misunderstanding, and I really want to be friends with you again, too.*

The corners of his mouth turned up, but he wasn't ready to commit to a full smile just yet. "Okay, cool, yeah, talk to management. Let me know what they say."

"I will," I said. "I totally will."

Ten seconds later, in front of the fish sticks, Jake said, "You can come over after school today if you want."

"Okay, cool. Sounds fun."

And just like that, we were friends again. Because that's how it works with middle school boys. Why talk about something uncomfortable when you can talk about French fries instead?

The other thing that happened is I kept working on the whole maturing thing. Meaning, I decided to "play by the rules" (Katie's words, not mine) and stop being my usual "obnoxious, annoying self." (George's words, not mine.) So I didn't drive the teachers as crazy as I used to. I didn't goof around in class as much as I used to. And I didn't brag about not reading, the way I used to.

Ms. Albone was the first teacher to notice it. "Charlie Joe," she said one day after class, "is everything all right?"

"Yes, Ms. Albone, why?"

"Well, I just realized that I haven't reprimanded you in a while."

"Right. Well, I, uh, have decided to try and be a little better behaved."

"I see." Ms. Albone looked at me closely, like she didn't quite believe it. "Well, good for you."

"Have a nice day, Ms. Albone."

Mrs. Sleep probably loved the new me. But I wasn't sure I did. Because honestly? I was worried that the new me was a little boring.

There was hope, though. The weather was getting nicer. The leaves were starting to bloom on the trees. You know what that means, right?

SUMMER.

Did you hear me? I said . . .

SUMMER.

You've heard of it, right? That time of year when there's absolutely no homework of any kind?

You can probably imagine how I felt about summer.

I WAS FOR IT.

Then one day, about a month before the last day of school, a bunch of us were sitting around at lunch talking about the end-of-year dance, which was a pretty big deal.

"Back where I come from," Emory said, "we all went to the beach and had a barbecue with surfing and volleyball. It was awesome, dudes."

"I'm totally moving to California when I grow up," Pete said.

"Uh-oh," said Jake. "Poor California."

"Charlie Joe, who are you going to take to the dance?" Timmy asked, a little too cheerfully. "Going solo?"

"Nope," I answered. "I'm taking Erica."

Emory's mouth dropped open. "You're taking Timmy's girlfriend?" The poor kid had a lot to learn about East Coast sarcasm.

"Very funny," Timmy said to me.

"Oh, now I'm with you! Good one dude," Emory said, chuckling.

Our conversation was interrupted by the crackling of

the loudspeaker, meaning an announcement was about to happen.

"Hello, students, this is your principal, Mrs. Sleep." As if we didn't all recognize her weird, deep voice. "This is a reminder: All permission slips for the field trip to the high school are due tomorrow. This applies to all students, no exceptions. Have a wise day." She always said that at the end of an announcement—*Have a wise day*. I wasn't exactly sure what it meant. Personally, I'd rather have a chocolate day, but that's just me.

Anyway, I'd forgotten about the field trip. All seventh and eighth graders visit the high school at the end of the year, to get used to the idea of going there one day. At the lunch table, everything got a little quiet for a minute. Nobody wanted to admit it, but we were all a little scared of the place.

"I've been there a few times," said Phil Manning. He had an older brother who was a sophomore. "It's huge."

"It's not so big," I reassured everyone. "I go there with Megan all the time." I'd never actually gone *inside* the building, but they didn't need to know that.

"From what I hear," said Jake, "it's almost like a college. So many extracurricular opportunities, and an incredible course selection."

He said that like it was a good thing, by the way. We all looked at him like he was from another planet, which of course he was.

"Well, all I know is, I'm perfectly happy right here," I said, speaking for pretty much everyone else at the table.

Or so I thought.

"Not me," said Nareem.

We all looked at him.

"Life is about embracing the unknown," he said.

I snorted. "Did you read that in a book somewhere?"

"As a matter of fact, I did," he said. And he held up a book.

A Communication Guide for Boys and Girls.

Until that moment, I had no idea you could actually physically feel your face turn red.

"Charlie Joe, are you okay?" Jake asked.

"Fine," I managed to choke out. "I think a fish stick went down the wrong way."

"Nareem," Katie said, "do you mind if I ask you why you're reading that book?"

"Yeah, no offense or anything, but that seems like a book only a loser would read," Timmy weighed in.

I felt my face go from red to green.

"I saw this book in the library," Nareem said. "Mrs. Reedy told me that someone else had just read it and found it quite fascinating. I looked through it, and it seemed like something I might benefit from. I am not embarrassed to say that I could use some improvement in that department."

The other kids all looked at Nareem, impressed that he could be so honest about it.

"In any case," he continued, "in the book, one is advised to take risks and to not be afraid. If you like a girl, or a boy, you should tell them."

"What does that have to do with high school?" I asked, trying to get us back to the original subject.

"Well," Nareem continued, "when we get to high school, it will be a similar situation. We must be ready to face all challenges. Whether it's a girl we like, or high school, or anything else for the rest of our lives."

"That sounds like good advice," Timmy said. "But the only challenge I'm really worried about is four hours of homework a night."

"Plus, I heard it takes you twenty minutes to walk from one end of the school to the other," Phil added.

"Can I see that book?" Katie asked Nareem.

He handed the book to her. She flipped to the very last page and started reading.

"*Every young person at some point faces the moment when he or she is ready to engage with a member of the opposite sex as a normal person, as opposed to acting as if they are different species. When that moment comes, it is important to remember that there is no special formula to boy-girl interaction. In fact, it is quite the opposite. It is ideal to make such communication not special at all: it should feel ordinary, an everyday occurrence, like talking to your friends. When boys and girls are able to speak normally with each other, without fear of being boring or dull; when they are able to sit quietly, and not feel like they have to fill every moment with conversation; when they are able to treat each other as one human being to another; then, and only then, will they have learned what it means to truly communicate.*"

Katie closed the book. Everyone sat quietly for a minute, thinking over what she had just read.

Finally I said, "I hope they have chocolate pudding in high school."

Katie smiled. "Stop feeling like you have to fill every moment with conversation," she said.

Bill Radonski's
Guide to Romance

STAY IN SHAPE!

As a gym teacher, I of course think that physical fitness is the root of all human happiness. Similarly, I find that the best way to connect with a woman is through exercise.

A nice long jog. A game of tennis. Spotting each other while lifting weights. Nothing helps two people bond more than seeing each other sweat.

Stay in shape, and romance is sure to follow. Remember—the heart is a muscle, too!

On the day of the high school field trip, I was late for school. Even though I had a good excuse—my mom couldn't find her keys, as usual—that still meant I was the last person on the bus.

Mr. Radonski was standing in the school parking lot as we pulled up.

"We've been waiting for you, Jackson," he said, pointing at his watch. "Are all the students supposed to be late for the high school because you couldn't get to school on time?"

"Sorry, Mr. Radonski," I said.

"SORRY DON'T FEED THE BULLDOG!" he yelled, whatever that means.

My mom popped out of her side of the car. "It's totally my fault, Bill," she said. "For the life of me, I couldn't find my car keys this morning!"

Mr. Radonski saw my mom, and his whole mood changed, of course. Apparently they'd gone to high school together, and I guess he had a thing for her—just writing that gives me the willies—so whenever he saw her he went from a pit bull to a puppy (something he'd never admit, by the way).

"Ah, Claire!" he said. "So good to see you, as always. Couldn't find the old keys, huh?"

"Sure couldn't," said my mom.

Mr. Radonski shook his head, but he was smiling. "Happens to me all the time, too. In this day and age you'd think they'd invent a way to live without keys, right?"

"Absolutely!" said my mom, flashing her nicest smile. She was no dummy—she knew a happy Mr. Radonski made my life a lot easier. "Well gotta run—have a great day, you two!"

I waved to my mom as she drove away. "Bye now!" hollered Mr. Radonski. "Always great to see you!" He kept waving until he noticed me looking at him. Then he looked a little embarrassed.

"You need to do a better job helping your mom find her keys in the morning," he told me. "Now get on that bus."

I hopped on the bus, and my worst fears were confirmed—no more seats, except for one.

In the very first row.

Next to the adult chaperone.

Who happened to be my old drama teacher, Mr. Twipple.

Just to remind you, Mr. Twipple and I had a complicated history. At first, we didn't get along too well, maybe because I used to imitate him by scrunching up my face to look more like a ferret than a person. (It was really funny until he found out about it. Then it was a lot less funny.) But then, I ended up playing the lead in this school play he wrote about the guy who invented paper towels, and he told me I was talented—even though I almost ruined the whole thing when I panicked on stage before kissing Hannah Spivero. Ever since then, we'd been pretty good pals. Even though I still thought he kind of looked like a ferret.

"Hey, Mr. Twipple," I said as I sat down next to him on the bus.

"Well hello, Charlie Joe." Mr. Twipple slid over to make room. "Excited about checking out the big campus?"

"I guess."

Mr. Twipple went back to reading his book—a biography of some guy named Marlon Brando—but two minutes later, he put it down. "Charlie Joe, can I ask you something?"

Uh-oh. "Sure."

"Well, I've noticed you haven't exactly been yourself lately," he said.

"What do you mean?"

"I mean, I've known you for a while now. We've had some good times and some bad times, but generally speaking, you're one of the liveliest personalities in school. It seems like lately, though, you've become a little more reserved. Is it just my imagination? Or is something going on with you?"

I shifted in my seat. "No, I'm good."

Mr. Twipple pointed at his book. "Charisma, Charlie Joe, is a rare thing. It's not something that can be taught—it's a gift. Most great performers have it. Marlon Brando, one of the finest American actors ever born, had it in spades." He slapped me on the knee. "You, Charlie Joe, have charisma. It's what makes you who you are, and it's what has allowed you to get away with many of the things you've gotten away with."

"Thanks. I think."

He chuckled. "You're welcome."

Two minutes later, I heard this come out of my mouth: "Have you ever liked a girl, but didn't know how to tell her, so you get this book about what to do, which ends up helping everyone else except you, and then when you end up trying to tell her, you mess it all up, and so now you don't know if you'll ever be able to tell her again?"

"As a matter of fact, that happened to me just last night," Mr. Twipple said.

"Really?"

"No."

"Oh."

Another minute went by, then my mouth said this: "Well, this book I read said that I shouldn't try so hard to be like the funniest kid all the time. That maybe I should just be more relaxed and normal and not show off so much by doing goofy things and stuff. So that's what I'm trying to do."

A nervous cheer went up as the bus turned into the high school parking lot.

"I'm sure this book was written by a very distinguished

author," Mr. Twipple said. "And I'm definitely no expert. But I will give you one small piece of advice."

The bus stopped, and someone smacked my shoulder. "Hey, Charlie Joe!"

I turned around to see Pete and Timmy standing there, waiting. "Come on, time to go!" Pete said.

"Yeah, man, let's go check out the high school," Timmy added.

I stayed in my seat. "Give me one second."

They both stared at me, shocked that I was still sitting there, having a serious conversation with a teacher. And not just any teacher—*Mr. Twipple*. "Fine," Pete said, "but hurry up."

As they piled off the bus, I turned back to Mr. Twipple. I could tell he was happy that I'd chosen him over my friends, if only for a minute. It turns out that teachers like to feel cool, too—and I had a hunch Mr. Twipple didn't feel cool all that often.

"What's your small piece of advice?"

"It's this," Mr. Twipple said. "Everyone has their own definition of normal. Your normal might not be someone else's normal. The important thing is to not be defined by what other people say you should be. If you do that, you're actually doing the opposite of being yourself. You're being who someone else wants you to be."

I sat there for a second, more confused than ever.

"You're not the quiet, polite type," he went on. "You're the master of the grand gesture. The bold move. So go for it! Do something grand and bold. Win the love of this girl!"

I grabbed my backpack and stood up. "Wait a second. So what you're saying is that I should go back to being the type of kid who drives teachers like you absolutely crazy?"

"God forgive me for saying this," Mr. Twipple said, "but exactly."

As we walked around the high

school, I realized two things:

1. My conversation with Mr. Twipple had put me in the best mood I'd been in for a while; and
2. High schools are pretty sweet.

First we went to the school gym, which had like nine basketball courts.

It was awesome.

Then we went to the auditorium, which looked like Radio City Music Hall compared to our middle school auditorium. They even let us stand on the stage.

It was awesome-er.

Then we went to watch some kids actually broadcast a live TV morning show from an actual TV studio!

It was totally beyond awesome.

By the time we got to the cafeteria, which actually had a soft-serve ice cream machine, kids were practically jumping up and down with excitement. High school didn't seem scary anymore. It seemed full of possibilities!

Then they had to go and ruin everything by taking us to the library.

"Holy smokes," Jake Katz said, in awe.

"Holy smokes," I said, in horror.

The high school library actually had two floors. Two floors! There were computer stations everywhere, which wasn't so bad, but there were also a lot of books. No, make that a TON of books. There were rows and rows and rows of books. There were way more books than any human being could ever read in ten lifetimes.

It was like the New York Public Library's little brother.

There was a biography section that was the size of a football field. A *biography* section! I'm sorry, but there is no way there are that many people in the world who deserve to have a book written about them.

A tall woman with glasses hanging around her neck came up to us with a big smile on her face. "Hello! I'm Ms. Cryer, and I'm the director of media services here at the high school."

I couldn't help it. I laughed.

"Do you mind if I ask you what is so funny?" Ms. Cryer asked.

I hesitated. The older old me would have made some goofy joke, but the newer old me would have just shook my head and been a good boy. But after my talk on the bus with Mr. Twipple, I decided that the newer old me should go back to the older old me.

That's logical, right?

"Well, I just think your name is kind of funny," I said.

Ms. Cryer cocked her head. "How so?"

"Well, it seems to make a lot of sense that someone who has to work in a huge library all day would have the word *cry* in her name."

Some kids giggled, which felt good. I'd missed that sound.

"I see," said Ms. Cryer. "So I gather you're not a fan of reading?"

"That's an understatement," Jake volunteered.

"Let's just say it's not in my top ten," I said.

Ms. Cryer walked over to a shelf, picked up a book, and walked over to me. "Here, hold this."

I took the book.

"This young man is holding one of over five thousand books we have in our library," Ms. Cryer announced to all the students. "And I am quite sure that before you have finished your time here, I can help each one of you find at least five books that you will read, enjoy, and learn from." Then she looked directly at me. "And as for you, young man, I will personally guarantee it."

I looked up at her. "You will?"

"Oh, yes," she said, still smiling. "In fact, I'll make you a bet. Name your terms." It seemed like she was having fun, and I began to think that when I got to high school, I might like her as much as I liked Mrs. Reedy. Why did I get along so great with librarians? It made absolutely no sense.

"Okay, fine," I said. "I'll bet you I won't read five books from this library during high school. If you win, I will read five more books over the summer between high school and college." I paused for a second. "And if I win, you have to move all these bookshelves out of the way so we can have a Ping-Pong tournament in here during the last week of school."

Ms. Cryer laughed. "You've got yourself a deal."

"Cool," Timmy said. "I love Ping-Pong."

We spent another hour checking out the whole school, which was totally huge of course, but also kind of amazing. To get from one class to another, sometimes you even got to walk outside. It was like college!

By the time we headed back to the buses, everyone was talking about how they couldn't wait to go to high school.

"Dude," said Emory, "I am totally stoked for this place."

"Is 'stoked' good?" Nareem asked.

Emory nodded enthusiastically. "Totally, dude."

The whole courtyard was filled with happy, chattering people, but I couldn't help noticing that one person wasn't participating in the fun.

Katie Friedman.

She was standing off to the side, talking to Mrs. Massey, our art teacher, who was another chaperone on the trip. I watched Katie for a few seconds, trying to decide if I wanted to know why she wasn't having fun. At first I thought it might have involved me. But then I decided that would be giving myself too much credit.

So I went over.

"Hey, Mrs. Massey," I said. "The art studios are pretty amazing here."

Mrs. Massey gave me a hug. She was a hugger. "Charlie Joe, so lovely to see you! Yes, indeed, this school is a painter's paradise. Professional artists all over the world would love to work in studios like these."

"I'll bet. Hey, how's Zoe?" Zoe Alvarez—my almost-girlfriend from the year before—happened to be her granddaughter.

"She's very well, Charlie Joe, very well indeed. So nice of you to ask."

"That's good." Well, enough small talk with Mrs. Massey. I turned to Katie. "Hey."

She gave a halfhearted smile. "Hey."

I casually pulled her away from Mrs. Massey to get a little privacy. "So, is everything okay? You don't seem all that into this place."

Katie looked down and stared at something on the ground that wasn't there. "No, this place is amazing," she said. "Totally incredible."

"So how come you don't look as psyched as everyone else?"

She picked her head up and looked at me for a split second, then looked up at the sky. "Well . . ." she said.

I was getting a weird feeling in my stomach. "Well what?"

Finally she looked at me straight on. "Well, I think I might actually go to private school next year."

My stomach did a weird somersault. "Private school?"

Katie nodded sadly. "Yup. My parents think it might be good for me. More challenges and all that."

"That's crazy! Our school is awesome!" I felt myself getting all worked up. "And did you see this place? It's incredible! It's got everything you could possibly want! It's like a college! Come on!"

"Listen, Charlie Joe, you don't have to convince me." Katie started walking to the bus, and I followed.

"So that's it, then? You're going off to private school, and we'll never see you again?"

"Don't be overdramatic. Of course we'll see each other. It's not as if I'm moving to another town, like Zoe did."

We both glanced back at Mrs. Massey, who was happily chatting with one of the art teachers from the high school.

"It won't be the same," I said. "It just won't."

And we walked the rest of the way to the bus in silence.

Hannah Spivero's
Guide to Romance

BRAINS ARE BEAUTIFUL.

Everyone is so concerned about looks all the time. I think that's really obnoxious. Looks are superficial. I like my boyfriend Jake not because he's cute, even though he totally, totally is—in a different kind of way—but because he's a really smart, interesting person. He knows a ton about a lot of things and teaches me stuff every day. And he says I teach him stuff, too. So, yeah, it's what's underneath that counts!

Although I am trying to get Jake to wear his contact lenses more. His eyes are like this really beautiful blue.

That day after school, Timmy, Jake, and I all went over to Pete's house. The original plan was to hang out and play video games, but I had something I needed to discuss first.

"Katie Friedman is going to private school next year," I announced.

They all looked up from their controllers.

"No way!" said Pete.

"Whoa," said Timmy.

"Sorry, Charlie Joe," said Jake.

Pete looked at Jake. "What do you mean, 'sorry Charlie Joe'?"

Jake looked at me, waiting. He was right—it was my question to answer.

"Listen, you guys," I said. "I suppose it's possible that I've been a little jealous that you guys all have girlfriends, and I don't. And I know it's also not exactly a shock that I like Katie."

They all gasped sarcastically.

"But the problem is, I've been having trouble figuring out how to tell her I like her," I went on. "I figured it was no big deal since there was no rush. But then today she told me she might go to private school." I sighed like a lovesick puppy. "So if you guys have any ideas about how to get her to not go, I'd really appreciate it."

"You mean, like a plan?" Pete said.

"Yeah. Like a plan."

Timmy snorted. "Wait a second. What happened to the new Charlie Joe, who's all nice and polite and wants totally to stay out of trouble?"

"Mr. Twipple told me that he didn't have charisma," I said.

"He didn't," Jake agreed.

Pete said, "I'm Googling 'how to get a girl to not go to private school.'"

"I don't think you can Google that," Timmy said.

Pete kept typing. "You can Google anything."

While we waited for Pete's phone to work its magic, Jake said, "And to think, I spent all that time worrying about you liking Hannah."

"I guess that's what's weird about girls," I said. "I did have the biggest crush on Hannah for like, forever. But I'm not sure I ever really *liked her* liked her. You know what I mean?"

"Not really," Jake said. And why would he? He liked liked *liked* Hannah.

"Hold on," Pete said. "I got something." He stood up for the big announcement.

"'Many private schools have strict codes of conduct.

They expect all applicants to have exceptional strength of character. Schools tend to look less favorably on applicants who have problems of discipline on their records.'"

We all sat there in silence for a minute, absorbing this information.

"So let me get this straight," Timmy said. "The best way to get Katie to not go to private school is to get her in trouble?"

"You'd have to do more than just get her in trouble," Jake said. "It has to be something that goes on her permanent record. Like, suspended."

"Whoa," I said. "Nice try. No way."

Timmy frowned. "So you're just going to let her go?"

"She'll be around for summers and stuff," I said, trying to look on the bright side. But I felt miserable just thinking about it.

"Hey!" said Pete. "The old Charlie Joe wouldn't accept that. The old Charlie Joe would have found a way to make it happen."

"To make what happen?" I said. "To get Katie suspended from school? Are you nuts?"

"Look, Charlie Joe, it's cool," Timmy said. "I get it. You like Katie. You don't want to do anything that might make her look bad."

"Guys, like I said, forget it," I told them. "She would, like, hate me for life. And for good reason. We need another plan."

We all stared into space for a few seconds, thinking.

"Hey, here's an idea," Jake said. "What if we fake the whole thing?"

We all said various versions of "Huh?"

Jake stood up and started pacing around the room, getting excited by his own idea. "It's simple. We do something to get Katie in a tiny bit of trouble, and then right when she gets caught, Charlie Joe immediately steps up and confesses to the whole thing, and he tells her that the whole reason he did it is because he likes her so much he wanted to get her in trouble so she wouldn't go to private school."

The rest of us scratched our heads like our hair hurt.

"I have no idea what you're talking about," I said.

Pete smacked his forehead. "Wait, I get it! Jake's saying we just get her in a tiny bit of trouble, but then you can say it was all to make sure she won't leave you by going to private school."

Jake looked at Pete. "You basically just repeated what I said."

"Cool," answered Pete.

"But I don't get it," I said. "If she doesn't actually get in trouble, then she'll still go to private school."

"So you want her to get in *real* trouble?" Jake asked.

"Of course not," I answered.

"Charlie Joe, think of it this way," Timmy said. "If you do this, you'll be her hero. She'll think it's like superromantic, and maybe she'll decide she can't go away because she won't want to leave you."

Pete made gross kissing noises. "Oh, Charlie Joe, my hero! I love you so much!"

"Ew," Jake said, but he was smiling, proud that he had come up with a plan that Pete and Timmy actually liked. Then he turned to me. "So what do you say?"

I thought about what they said. Things between Katie and I were okay, I guess. We were definitely friends again, but like I said before, something wasn't quite right. It wasn't like it was before all this stuff happened, that's for sure. Talking to her had become kind of stressful. I was a little hung up on the private school thing. And it was entirely possible she was still hung up on the kissing-Hannah thing.

So overall, we were at like a B-minus. Which is a grade

I would have been perfectly satisfied with if we were talking about, say, Social Studies.

But we're talking about Katie Friedman. And I wanted an A.

"You really think she would think that *me* getting *her* in trouble would be romantic?" I asked.

Jake shrugged, then nodded. "After getting over the initial shock? Probably."

Huh. Well, if Jake thought so . . .

"What did you guys have in mind exactly?" I asked.

They all looked at each other.

"That's where you come in," Jake said.

We sat there and thought for another minute.

"It has to be something funny," I said. "Something that gets her in a little bit of trouble, maybe not enough to actually get her rejected from private school, but something that all the kids would think was awesome. And then I could immediately confess and say I only did it because I like her, and I don't want her to go to private school."

"Why does everyone just keep repeating exactly what I said?" asked Jake.

I thought for another minute.

"Okay, let's do it," I said.

"Sweet!" Pete hollered. Then, a minute later, he added, "Do what?"

"I have no idea," I said.

Which is when Pete's mom stuck her head in and said, "Pete, don't forget to restock the henhouse."

Which is when I remember that Pete's family raised chickens.

Which is when a lightbulb went off in my head.

Call it fate, call it good timing, call it bad timing, call it whatever you want—but as Pete groaned and headed outside, I called to him, "Hey, Pete? Can I ask you something?"

He turned back. "What?"

I hesitated, then decided to go for it.

"Have any of your chickens ever been on a road trip?"

For the next three weeks, it was business as usual. People started getting more and more excited as the school year started winding down. Then, on the first day of the last week of school, we had an awards ceremony. Jake got a Math award for figuring out some equation that hadn't been solved since 1794 (okay, that's a slight exaggeration, but it was a really hard equation). Pete Milano got an Art award for an incredible drawing of two basset hounds. And Katie got a special award from the English department for being the best writer in the grade. Her acceptance speech was an amazing poem that rhymed *munificence* with *benevolence*—two words I had never heard before and haven't heard since. They probably don't even *know* those words at private school.

I didn't get an award, by the way. Can you believe it?

The day after the awards ceremony, I texted Pete.

What's up? Dance is in three days. Are we all set?

He texted back a picture of a chicken and these words: **Meet Cletus.**

Game on.

Cletus

That day at lunch, all anybody wanted to talk about was the year-end dance.

"Charlie Joe, still not going with anybody?" Eliza asked me.

"Nope," I said.

Eliza smiled. After all these years, she still enjoyed knowing I was girlfriendless.

"Erica's dad is driving us to the dance in his cool Alfa Romeo convertible," Timmy bragged. I had no idea what an Alfa Romeo was—I don't know anything about cars—but it was still annoying.

Then Katie came running up, beaming. "Hey, guess what you guys? I just found out we can play at the dance!" No wonder she was so excited. Her band, CHICKMATE, was pretty much the most important thing in her life. Earlier in the year, she'd even gotten Jane Plantero from Plain Jane to sing one of her songs at the talent show. But Katie had always wanted to play at a school dance, and she was finally going to get her chance.

As everyone congratulated Katie and said things like "That's awesome!" and "So cool!" and "You rock!" it dawned on me that there was one small problem with this wonderful news.

Cletus.

I immediately texted Pete, who was sitting two tables away.

Hold on. Maybe we should forget plan

He texted back.

Why?

I texted back.

Katie's band is playing

He texted back.

That's okay. Chickens love music, trust me!

I got a slightly sickening feeling in my stomach, but I ignored it. I texted back.

Okay

Moral of the story: Never trust your friends.

35

The last day of school is more like a party than a school day. All the books have been put away for the year, and everybody is excited about the dance, and signing each other's yearbooks, and talking about the summer. If every day were like the last day of the year, school would be the most awesome place on earth.

As usual, I made sure a bunch of teachers signed my yearbook. They wrote some awesome things.

I ENJOYED HAVING YOU IN MY GYM CLASS, EVEN THOUGH YOU DROVE ME ABSOLUTELY CRAZY. KEEP WORKING OUT!
—MR. RADONSKI
P.S. TELL YOUR MOM I SAY HI!

Charlie Joe:
You are an interesting young man. Sometimes, even in a good way. ☺ But seriously, you are one of a kind, and I have complete faith in you.
DON'T LET ME DOWN!
Love, Ms. Ferrell

I've enjoyed getting to know you. You're a fine young man. And an even better fox hunter.
Take care,
Mrs. Massey

P.S. Zoe says hi!

Bravo, Mr. Jackson! Remember to keep acting . . . as opposed to acting out! And remember: Charisma is a gift. Use it wisely.
Theatrically yours,
Benjamin Twipple

You're a Really Excellent Awesome Dude. (READ, get it?)
Your library pal, Mrs. Reedy

When I asked Mrs. Sleep to sign it, at first she shook her head. She said, "Mr. Jackson, if I signed your yearbook, I might write something I would later regret." Then she winked at me, grabbed my pen and wrote, *You have a lot to offer the world. I just hope the world is ready for it. Good luck. Mrs. Sleep.*

You know something? Mrs. Sleep is a pretty cool lady after all.

36

That night, I picked at my food.

"Are you nervous about the dance, honey?" my mom asked at dinner.

"Of course not!" I said, but she knew I was lying. It was a well-known fact in my family that I always got nervous before these kinds of things, because I was a lousy dancer.

I ate quietly and looked down at my two dogs. Moose, my hero, was watching me patiently. He knew his turn would come, and I'd give him my plate to lick. Coco was napping right next to him. She always let Moose take lookout. But when the time came, she'd be right there with him, fighting over every scrap.

I noticed Moose was getting a gray beard. It was really cute, but it made me sad, too. I didn't like being reminded that he was getting older. I wish dogs never got older.

Megan wasn't home, so it was just my mom and me at first. Halfway through dinner, my dad came home. As soon as he walked through the door, I saw my mom's eyes change. It was like a light went on inside them. It may have happened every night when Dad came home, but that night, I really noticed it. She jumped up and walked to the door. And my dad's eyes, when he saw my mom, lit up the same way.

My dad kissed my mom, and they hugged.

"How was work?" my mom asked.

"Gripping," my dad said. Mom laughed, because he was kidding.

"How was school?" my dad asked. My mom was taking some classes at the local university.

"Excellent, actually," she said. "I'm really impressed with one of my professors."

"Good news," said my dad. "He's probably impressed with you, too. You're going to make a terrific therapist."

As he sat down and started eating, I noticed something I'd never noticed before. He held his fork with his left hand and my mom's hand with his right hand. And the amazing thing was, it seemed like he didn't even know he was doing it. Every once in a while, he would let go of my mom's hand to pick up the knife and cut something. But as soon as he was done, he'd grab her hand again.

It reminded me of how when they watched TV together, they sat really close to each other, always touching just a little bit, even though the couch was big.

And it also reminded me of how my mom twirled her hair sometimes when she was talking to my dad on the phone, almost like she was back in high school or something.

"Charlie Joe?" I suddenly heard my dad say. "Everything okay there, buddy?"

I snapped back to reality and looked at my parents. They'd known each other forever, probably like twenty years or something. They really, *really* loved each other. And the most amazing thing about it was that they didn't have to shout about it. They didn't have to brag about it. And they definitely didn't have to bring chickens to school dances to prove it.

They just did.

Which made me suddenly realize what I had to do.

I jumped out of my chair. "Um, yeah, I'm good, Dad," I said. "Can I be excused?"

My mom looked confused, but she nodded. "Sure, honey."

I ran up the stairs two at a time and texted Pete and Timmy.

Dudes! Cancel plan! Cancel chicken! Cancel everything!

Timmy texted back.

Why?

I answered.

Because I have a new plan. It's called just being myself.

Timmy texted.

Well that sounds like a lame plan. Plus, Pete got his phone taken away by his mom for using his bedspread as a napkin.

Uh-oh.

I'm leaving now to find Pete! But if this doesn't go well, forward my mail to Timbuktu.

Jim Jackson's Guide to Romance

MAKE 'EM LAUGH.

A couple of weeks ago, I forgot to take out the garbage, and in the middle of the night, the dogs decided to distribute it throughout most of the house. The next morning, my wife, Claire, was so mad. So I did the only thing I could think of. I made a joke. It wasn't the best joke in the world—to tell you the truth, I can't even remember what it was. But Claire laughed, a little. Don't get me wrong, she was still mad. But she was mad while smiling.

It's true, funny guys get away with murder. So do funny girls. So sharpen that sense of humor. Trust me, you're gonna need it.

And if you're anything like me, you're gonna need it A LOT.

"Mom! We gotta go! Now!"

"Coming, honey," she said, way too casually, as I dragged her out the door. On the way to the car, I picked a few flowers from the garden and wrapped them up in a rubber band. Just in case.

I hid them from my mom, of course—she probably would have been mad. She loved her flowers.

I managed to get there just as the dance was starting. The theme was "Friendship Is the Best Ship," and there were posters all over the walls of kids from the class, but we were Photoshopped as if we were standing on different kinds of boats—sailboats, motorboats, battleships, etc. There was a picture of Katie and me, and they made it look as if we were standing on a canoe. The caption underneath said CAREFUL, DON'T TIP OVER!

CAREFUL! DON'T TIP OVER!

Katie was already on stage with her band, CHICK-MATE. Did I mention that they are really good? They are. I was pretty positive she was going to be famous one day.

But enough about Katie Friedman, rock star. I had to find Pete and Timmy. I looked all over the entire school and finally found them behind the stage. Pete was carrying what looked like a giant Easter basket. And sure enough, the basket was moving.

"Is that Cletus in there?" I whispered.

"Yup," Pete said. "Wanna meet him?"

"No! You need to get him out of here! I want to cancel the whole thing!"

Pete stared at me. "What do you mean? I brought him all the way here! You can't just cancel!"

"Yes, I can!"

"I don't get you, Charlie Joe. It's your plan!"

"Well, it was Jake's plan to make the plan," I said. Speaking of Jake, I noticed he was nowhere to be found. How convenient for him.

"But it's so simple!" Pete protested. "All we're going to do is put the basket next to Katie's jacket and then spread the word that Katie brought a chicken to the school dance, and then Mrs. Sleep or Mr. Radonski or some other teacher will find out, and then Mrs. Sleep will ask Katie if she brought a chicken to school, and then Katie will deny it, and then Mrs. Sleep will ask her if she's telling the truth, and then Katie will start to get upset and maybe even cry, and that's when you step in and say it was all your idea, you wanted to get her in trouble so she wouldn't go away to private school, because you like her and want to marry her and live happily ever after."

Timmy and I stared down at the basket, then up at Pete.

"When you put it like that, it doesn't actually sound that simple," I said.

"The whole thing will all be over in like five minutes," Pete added. "What's the problem?"

But I never had the chance to tell Pete what the problem was, because at that very moment, Sammie Corcoran started her drum solo. Which involved a lot of cymbals.

And as it turns out, chickens are not big fans of cymbals.

When Sammie hit her third cymbal crash, Cletus decided he'd had enough. And before anyone knew what was happening, he pecked the flaps of the basket open and took off.

Timmy, Pete, and I looked at each other. Pete said, "That's not good"—which was the understatement of the year—and then we all took off after the chicken.

"Hey, get back here!" I shouted, just in case Cletus knew English.

Meanwhile, Katie was still playing, her eyes closed, singing her heart out. Coincidentally enough, they were playing a song called "Chick Power," which Katie wrote.

All the little chicks with all their little beaks/Gonna take back the night and take back the streets! It was actually a really cool, intense song about girls and women fighting for respect in a male-dominated world. Unfortunately, the only thing people remember about it now is that it was the song Katie's band was playing when a chicken ran across the stage, jumped down onto the dance floor, flapped its way over to Mrs. Sleep, and pooped on her shoes.

You know that expression "I saw my life flash before my eyes?" Right at that moment, I realized it wasn't a figure of speech. But of course, everyone thought it was hilarious. Kids started howling with laughter, as Mrs. Sleep stared down at her soiled footwear. Meanwhile, the chicken clucked happily and scampered away.

Mrs. Sleep roared, "IS THIS SOMEONE'S IDEA OF A JOKE?!"

That got the band's attention. They stopped playing. Katie opened her eyes and saw Cletus running around the dance floor. She looked shocked, which was probably the only predictable thing that happened the whole night.

Here are just a few of the highlights from the next five minutes:

People chased Cletus all over the gym.

Cletus drank some punch.

Cletus ate half of a cupcake.

Cletus trampled over all the other cupcakes.

Ms. Albone, my English teacher, dove on the floor trying to catch Cletus, but missed and tore her dress. She was wearing pink underwear that night, in case you were wondering.

Cletus ran back onto the stage and knocked over one of Sammie Corcoran's cymbals. (I told you he wasn't a fan.) Sammie screamed and threw one of her drumsticks at Cletus. It missed and hit poor Nareem in the leg. He jumped back in surprise and spilled his drink all over Mrs. Sleep, who was kneeling down, trying to scrape the poop off her shoes.

I guess what I'm trying to say is, it was a pretty busy five minutes.

Finally, it seemed like Cletus had had enough. He headed back toward his basket, but on the way, he knocked over Katie's guitar case, which was in

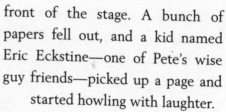

front of the stage. A bunch of papers fell out, and a kid named Eric Eckstine—one of Pete's wise guy friends—picked up a page and started howling with laughter.

"Look!" he screamed. "I found one of Katie's songs! Listen to this!"

He jumped up on the stage and went right up to the microphone.

"'Charlie Joe Jackson Has a Pimple on His Fanny,'" Eric announced. "A song by Katie Friedman."

Wait, *WHAT?!*

My entire body suddenly felt like it was on fire. I looked at Katie, like, *huh?* She looked like she wanted to jump out a window.

Mr. Twipple ran up to Eric. "Give me that!" He tried to snatch it out of Eric's hands, and a few other teachers tried to grab it, too, but Eric was too quick. He began to read Katie's "song" at the top of his lungs.

Poor Charlie Joe, in case you didn't know,
he has a pimple on his fanny.
When he tries to sit, it hurts a little bit, coz he
has a pimple on his fanny.

He always picks it, thinking that might fix it,
but it turns out to not be all that simple.
Charlie Joe Jackson's fanny has a big, fat
    pimple!

Meanwhile, I finally remembered how to work my legs. I ran up behind Eric while he was high-fiving his friends, and tackled him.

"OW!" Eric screamed.

"Give me that!" I shouted, trying to snatch the piece of paper out of his hand. "Give me that right now!"

I felt a hand on my shoulder. "I'll handle this," Ms. Ferrell said. "I'll take that," she said to Eric calmly. He handed it over.

Meanwhile, Mr. Twipple came up to us, dragging Timmy and Pete by their arms. Pete was holding the basket.

"I found them out in the parking lot with the chicken, trying to call a taxi," Mr. Twipple explained.

"This whole chicken thing was Charlie Joe's idea!" Timmy wailed, throwing me under the bus as usual.

By this time, a bunch of other kids and adults had come up behind us. "Mr. Jackson?" rumbled Mrs. Sleep. "Is this true? Are you behind these very unfortunate events? And if so, why would you do such a thing?"

But before I even had a chance to answer, Mrs. Sleep turned her attention to Katie. "And did you really write that song? I must say, Miss Friedman, that I'm surprised.

Very, very surprised indeed." Mrs. Sleep shook her head at the two of us. "I'm going to call your parents. When they arrive, we'll discuss where to go from here."

Katie and I stood there, staring at each other. I thought for a second how crazy it was that I'd only wanted to *pretend* to get her in trouble, but now she actually *was* in trouble.

And then I thought back on everything that had happened over the last few months. And I realized I'd made everything too complicated, like always.

And I decided I had only one plan left.

I wasn't going to try and be funny. I wasn't going to try and be charismatic. I wasn't going to try and be nice. I wasn't going to try and be the rascal or the Goody Two-shoes. I wasn't going to try and be anything.

I was just going to be me.

The first thing I did was run up to the microphone that Katie had been singing into just a few minutes earlier.

"I'd like to say a few words."

My face was bright red, and I was sweating right through my shirt, but I didn't care. There was something I had to say.

"I remember when Jake Katz stood up on this same stage and told you all that he had read my books for me for the position paper. I remember how bad I felt about that, and how I promised myself I'd never be that embarrassed again. Well, here I am, just as embarrassed by what happened here today."

I stopped talking, just long enough to hear how silent it was in that room. The only thing you could hear was the buzzing coming out of Katie's amplifier.

"A couple of months ago, I went to the library to ask Mrs. Reedy for a book." Everyone giggled at that, like I knew they would. "I wanted a book that would teach me what I needed to know to get a girlfriend. I had never had a girlfriend, but there was a girl I liked, and I thought maybe she liked me back. But I wasn't sure." I looked all over the room, but I didn't look at Katie. Not yet. "The book was interesting, but I ended up helping other kids more than myself. It seemed like everything I tried ended up going wrong. And I said and did some things that made the girl I liked mad at me for a long time."

Now, finally, I was ready. I looked right at her. She looked right back at me.

"Finally, after a lot of crazy mistakes, I realized that I didn't need to read any books or play any tricks to get her to like me back. I just needed to be myself. But then this girl told me she might be going to private school next year. And that got me really upset. And I would do anything for her not to go to private school." I paused. "Even get her in a little trouble by making it seem like she brought a live chicken to school. And I'm really, really sorry about that."

A little gasp went up from the crowd, as people waited to see what I was going to do next. I hopped off the stage and walked up to Katie.

"The book I read was called *A Communication Guide for Boys and Girls*, and it came out like a zillion years ago. I think someone needs to write a new book, called HOW TO TALK TO GIRLS LIKE A NORMAL PERSON. Maybe I'll write it. If I did, the first sentence would be, 'If you like a girl, just tell her.' And the last sentence would be 'Just be yourself, and hope for the best.' So here goes."

I handed her the flowers that, amazingly enough, were still in my hand. "I like you, Katie Friedman. I like you a lot. In fact, I think I've always liked you. Ever since I first met you. I just didn't know it."

Some kid yelled, "Yeah!"

Another kid yelled, "About time!" and everyone laughed.

Then it was silent.

Katie bent her head down to smell the flowers and stayed there for like ten seconds. The suspense was killing me. Finally she brought her head back up.

"I'm really sorry, too," Katie said, so softly that only I could hear her. "I'm really sorry that I wrote that song about your fanny. It was mean and stupid. But it was never, ever meant to be shown to anyone. I just did it as a private joke, to make myself feel better." It was her turn to take a deep breath. "Because you're right. I *was* mad at you. I was mad at you because I really, really liked you, too, but everything kept messing it up."

When she said that, it was like an ocean of relief and happiness filled my body.

Katie grabbed the microphone. "I think I spent most of the last five years telling myself that best friends can't be boyfriend and girlfriend," she told the crowd.

Then she smiled—a small, but incredibly real smile.

And she said, "Well, I've changed my mind."

And all of a sudden, I kissed Katie Friedman.

And she kissed me back.

And people started cheering.

* * *

Which is when I realized something. When two people need to stand there and think about whether or not they should kiss each other, then maybe it just might not be the right thing to do. But when they don't even think about it—when something just *makes* them start to kiss—then you know it's perfect.

So there I was, kissing Katie Friedman at long last, in what was probably the greatest moment of my life, when I felt something tickling my feet. I looked down.

SQUAWK!

Cletus was back.

"I'll get him!" Mr. Radonski yelled. He ran up and dove onto the floor, but the chicken scampered away. As I helped Mr. Radonski up, he looked at me and said, "Just FYI, I myself used to have a few pimples on my fanny, but I haven't for years. It's all about excellent hygiene."

"Good to know," I said.

We all watched as the chicken jumped up onto the food table and started helping himself to some Doritos. People thought it was hilarious. Then he decided he was full and started walking toward the sweets tray.

Two seconds later, there was a loud scream.

"He's peeing on the rice crispy treats!" someone hollered.

Needless to say, that didn't go over well.

"THAT'S ENOUGH!" screamed Mrs. Sleep. Moving as fast as I'd ever seen her move, she sprinted over to the refreshments, snatched Cletus while he was mid-pee, put him under her arm like a football, and marched over to Pete Milano.

"Mr. Milano, do you mind telling us all where you got this bird?" she thundered.

Pete tried to talk, but his mouth wasn't working very well. "My henhouse," he finally sputtered.

At first Mrs. Sleep looked surprised by that fact, but then she decided it wasn't worth the effort.

She let out a long sigh. "Well, let's go call your parents, too," Mrs. Sleep said to Pete, "because you've got a lot of explaining to do." Then she gave Katie and me a look. "I'll be chatting with you two later."

And out they marched: Pete, Mrs. Sleep, and Cletus.

I felt someone behind me, and I turned around to see Mr. Twipple standing there, with a nervous look on his face.

"That little chat we had on the bus, when I told you about how if you really wanted something you had to go for it and make a grand gesture. You didn't tell anybody about that, did you?"

I shook my head. "No, sir, Mr. Twipple."

He let out a relieved sigh. "Thank God for small favors," he said.

You know how when you've been thinking about something for, like, forever? And how you practically can't think of anything else, because you want it so badly? And then, when you actually finally get it, you can't believe it, and so you just stand there like a moron, because you don't know what to do?

Imagine that times ten, and you'll know how I felt, standing in the middle of the dance floor, staring at Katie Friedman.

As the party slowly returned to normal, some kids came up to Katie and me and congratulated us for finally realizing what everyone else seemed to know all along: that we were two of the dumbest people on earth for not realizing (or not admitting) that we liked each other. Timmy, Jake, Eliza, and Hannah knew. Mr. Twipple and Ms. Ferrell knew. Even Emory and Mareli knew, and they were the new kids in town.

I think I was in some kind of shock. I had known this girl for so long—more than half my life, when you think about it—and to finally know she was my girlfriend was the weirdest feeling in the world.

Just to *have* a girlfriend was the weirdest feeling in the world!

Katie was staring at me, too, but it didn't seem like she was in the slightest bit of shock at all. In fact, she looked like she was expecting this moment all along. I think that's probably the most fascinating thing of all about girls. They can be really dramatic, and emotional, and yeah, a little crazy, but when it comes right down to it, I think they're a lot wiser than boys. They just *get it*, you know? Meanwhile, boys are clueless. We just are. Hey, I'm the first to admit it!

And you know what? I'm okay with it.

"Are we just going to stand here and stare at each other all night?" Katie asked me.

"Um, I, uh . . ."

She laughed. "Well put."

We stood there for a few more seconds.

"Do you think I might get in trouble because of the chicken?" I asked.

Katie giggled a little. "Um, YEAH." Then a second later she said, "Do you think I might get in trouble because of the fanny song?"

I shook my head. "Actually, no," I said. "That's like an invasion of privacy or something. And free speech. You're totally off the hook."

"Well, listen to Mr. Legal Expert," Katie said, and we both laughed.

Then a slow song came on.

Uh-oh.

Katie looked at me and waited, but I just stood there. Then she smiled, took my arms, and placed them on her shoulders.

"Am I going to have to do everything in this relationship?" she asked.

"Maybe," I said.

We started to slow dance. Katie closed her eyes. After about ten seconds, she rested her head on my shoulder.

"Do you still think you're going to private school?" I whispered.

"I don't know," she whispered back.

A few seconds later, I closed my eyes, too.

✳ ✳ ✳

I wasn't sure how long Katie and I would go out. Maybe for the rest of our lives, maybe for the rest of the summer, maybe for the rest of the week. Who knows? The world is complicated. There's a lot to figure out, every day. But sometimes, the best thing to do is not worry about any of it.

Sometimes, the best thing to do is just close your eyes and dance.

How to Talk to Girls Like a Normal Person:

THE SHORTEST BOOK EVER WRITTEN
By Charlie Joe Jackson

Page 1—If you like a girl, tell her.

Page 2—Just be yourself and hope for the best.

The End

ACKNOWLEDGMENTS

Thanks to everyone at Roaring Brook Press/ Mackids. And a special shout-out to Lauren Burniac, who got shipped off to Planet Greenwald without a return ticket, and who is using her wit and wisdom to help me raise a new colony of books.

GOFISH

TOMMY GREENWALD

© Suzanne Sheridan

What did you want to be when you grew up?
I don't remember, but it probably involved chocolate.

Were you a reader or a non-reader growing up?
I was a reader. My kids still haven't forgiven me.

When did you realize you wanted to be a writer?
Who said anything about wanting to be a writer? I wanted to be a television watcher.

What's your most embarrassing childhood memory?
Ages six through thirteen.

What's your favorite childhood memory?
Hitting every ice cream store in town with my grandmother. (Who's still alive, by the way—ninety-nine and counting.)

As a young person, who did you look up to most?
Everybody. I was a pretty short kid.

What was your favorite thing about school?
Making jokes in class that made kids laugh.

What was your least favorite thing about school?
Getting in trouble for making jokes in class that made kids laugh.

What were your hobbies as a kid? What are your hobbies now?
Then: Playing with dogs. Now: Owning dogs.

What was your first job, and what was your "worst" job?
I taught archery one year at summer camp. I'd never held a bow and arrow in my life. By the end of the summer, I still hadn't.

How did you celebrate publishing your first book?
By calling my wife and attempting to speak.

Where do you write your books?
The train, the library, Barnes & Noble. Anywhere but home. Home is for television and dogs.

What is the one tip you would give to yourself in middle school?
Making the class laugh isn't necessarily the way to a teacher's heart.

What is the one tip you would give to kids currently in middle school?
Enjoy it while it lasts.

Which is better: extra sleep or extra food?
Both. Extra food, then extra sleep.

Which is extra better: extra-long summer vacation or an extra-long massage?
There's absolutely NOTHING better than an extra-long massage.

Which is worse: extra chores or extra homework?
Ugh. I get chills just thinking about both of them. I'm going to go with extra chores, since that's a lifetime sentence.

Which is extra worse: getting up extra early in the morning or picking up extra doggie doo-doo?
Dogs can do no wrong in my book, so I'll say getting up extra early.

What challenges do you face in the writing process, and how do you overcome them?
My desire to not work. When my guilt overcomes my laziness, I write.

Which of your characters is most like you?
Charlie's father.

What makes you laugh out loud?
The Daily Show.

What do you do on a rainy day?
Give thanks. An excuse not to exercise.

What's your idea of fun?
Watching my kids try their hardest at something.

What's your favorite song?
Depends on the week. This week? "I'm So Sick of You" by Cake.

Who is your favorite fictional character?
Fielding Mellish.

What was your favorite book when you were a kid? Do you have a favorite book now?
Then: *Are You My Mother?* by P. D. Eastman. Now: *Letting Go* by Philip Roth.

What's your favorite TV show or movie?
So many!! TV: *All in the Family, M*A*S*H, The Honeymooners, The Twilight Zone*, for starters. Movies: *Love and Death, Manhattan, The Shining.*

If you were stranded on a desert island, who would you want for company?
My family, as long as there was a desert school I could send the kids to.

If you could travel anywhere in the world, where would you go and what would you do?
Africa to go on safari. Someday.

If you could travel in time, where would you go and what would you do?
Eighteenth-century Vienna, to look over Mozart's shoulder when he was nineteen and writing incredible music.

What's the best advice you have ever received about writing?
My friend and agent Michele Rubin told me to change Charlie Joe's story from a picture book idea to a middle-grade novel.

What advice do you wish someone had given you when you were younger?
Stop eating Häagen-Dazs when you turn forty.

Do you ever get writer's block?
Nope.

What do you want readers to remember about your books?
That books aren't the enemy.

What would you do if you ever stopped writing?
Feel guilty.

What do you like best about yourself?
My family.

What do you consider to be your greatest accomplishment?
Charlie, Joe, and Jack.

What do you wish you could do better?
Sleep.

What would your readers be most surprised to learn about you?
I'm the fifth funniest person in my family.

Graduation day is here!

Charlie Joe has been looking forward to it, but then again, maybe being a kid isn't so bad after all.

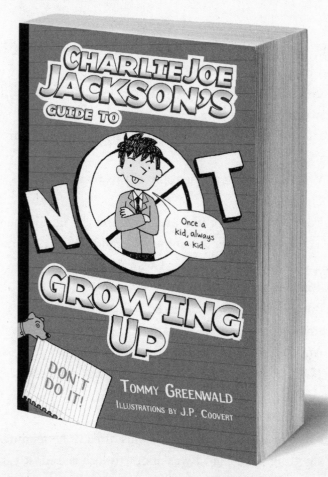

Keep reading for an excerpt.

INTRODUCTION

My name is Charlie Joe Jackson, and I used to hate reading.

Guess what? Now I hate it a little less. (Let's keep that between us.)

I guess that's what they call part of "the maturing process."

Which brings us to the topic of this book.

Growing up.

I used to be all for it. I used to think the idea of being an adult was totally awesome—I could drive a car, and play video games whenever I wanted, and watch movies that my parents won't let me watch now.

But then one day I realized—that's *crazy*. What was I thinking?

And when I say "one day," I mean, one actual day.

The day I realized that being a kid was the best job in the world.

The day I decided to *not* grow up.

I had to act fast, because it was already happening. I was getting older, and I was about to lose the most carefree part of my life. Forever!

You don't have to tell me it was a crazy idea, I know

that already. Childhood is fleeting, nothing lasts forever—blah blah blah. Trying to stop time is impossible, right?

Wrong.

When it came to growing up, I wasn't going down without a fight.

* * *

So anyway, not like I'm making excuses or anything, but hopefully that helps explain why, at exactly 5:51 on a lovely spring evening, there was a graduation ceremony happening at Eastport Middle School, with 183 students scheduled to graduate, but only 182 of them were present.

Want to guess who was missing?

Yup. You got it. Me.

Instead, there I was, sitting in a dark room by myself, wondering what the heck happened—and if it was somehow my fault, as usual.

There was a knock on the door.

"Charlie Joe? Are you in there?"

I closed my eyes and sighed. I wasn't exactly in the mood to see anybody right at that moment.

Oh, yeah—one more thing I forgot to mention.

It was my birthday.

Part One

LET'S GO BACK TO THE BEGINNING, SHALL WE?

"Yes!" I said to myself, as my eyes opened for the first time that morning.

Which, I can honestly say, had never happened before. Usually, the first words I say when I wake up are "Go away," and it comes out sounding more like "Murfle-blorg."

But this was a morning different from any other. This, people, was a morning that I had been looking forward to ever since my mother first dragged me kicking and screaming to the school bus way back when. (I think you can still see the skid marks from my shoes at the bus stop.)

First of all, like I said, it was my birthday. Already a reason to celebrate, right?

But there was more—much, much more. Because this was the morning of the day I was graduating from Eastport Middle School. The first day of the rest of my life. The day I put the past behind me—all my crazy behavior and silly ideas and goofy troublemaking ways—and started acting like a mature person.

Or not.

I flipped over on the bed and reached for my phone, which was charging on the nightstand. I liked to sleep with my phone close by, and by close by, I mean approximately three inches away.

I texted my friend group—which included Timmy, Jake, Pete, and Nareem—two simple words: **Today! Yeah!**

Timmy texted back: **See you at Jakes noon.**

Nareem texted back: **Very much looking forward to it.**

Pete texted back: **Rockin' high school baby.**

Jake texted back: **If you guys break anything in my house i'll kill you.**

I was about to settle in for a nice long text war when there was a soft knock on the door.

"Honey?"

My mom poked her head in. She had a big blue balloon in her hand.

"Oh, hey, Mom," I said, putting my phone away. I didn't need her to start in with the you're-on-that-thing-too-much speech. There would be plenty of time for that later in the day. And for the rest of my life.

She kissed me on the cheek. "Happy birthday! Can you believe it? A birthday and a graduation all in one day!"

"Totally!" I said. "Although I do feel like I'm kind of getting ripped off. It would be nice to spread them out a little bit."

"I get that," Mom said.

I sat up in bed. "But, yeah, this is basically the best day of my life. No more middle school!"

"I thought you liked middle school."

"I guess so," I said, shrugging. Sometimes it's hard to explain to parents that you can like something but still want to never do it again. Sure, middle school *was* fun, but by the end, enough was enough, right? Time to move on.

"I better get going," I added, stretching. "Lots to do." But my mom wasn't moving. She was just sitting there, on the edge of my bed. This was weird—usually she had to beg me just to get up.

"Mom?"

"Yes, honey?"

"Like I said, I think I should probably get up."

She sighed. "It all goes by so fast."

"What does?"

"All of it." Then she took a tissue out of her pocket and blew her nose, which was also weird, since she never has a runny nose. "Megan's about to go to college. You're going off to high school. And you were both born yesterday."

"Yesterday?"

She smacked me on the head with a pillow. "Not literally yesterday," she said. "You're too young to get it, but time . . . you blink and the years fly by, just like that."

That was when I realized that my mom was blowing her nose because she was crying a little bit.

"Don't be sad!" I said. "I'm not going anywhere! And neither is Megan! We love home! Home is awesome!"

"I know, sweetheart." She smiled, but it seemed like part of the smile wasn't actually there. "It's just that these big milestone days, they're not easy on a mother. It was hard your first day of kindergarten, and it's hard now." She wiped her eyes one last time, then got up and went to the door. "See you downstairs, birthday-graduation boy."

All Charlie Joe.
All the time.

THE CHARLIE JOE JACKSON SERIES

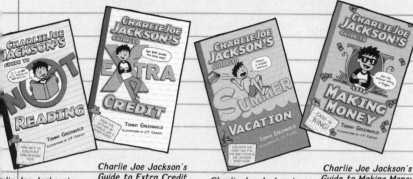

Charlie Joe Jackson's
Guide to Not Reading
ISBN: 978-1-59643-691-6

Charlie Joe Jackson's
Guide to Extra Credit
ISBN: 978-1-250-01670-6

Charlie Joe Jackson's
Guide to Summer Vacation
ISBN: 978-1-59643-757-9

Charlie Joe Jackson's
Guide to Making Money
ISBN: 978-1-250-10716-9

Charlie Joe Jackson's
Guide to Planet Girl
ISBN: 978-1-59643-841-5

Charlie Joe Jackson's
Guide to Not Growing Up
ISBN: 978-1-626-72169-2

Pete Milano's Guide
to Being a Movie Star
ISBN: 978-1-626-72167-8

Voted the best
books ever!
cjjbookshelf.com
mackids.com

Katie Friedman Gives Up Texting!
(And Lives to Tell About It.)
ISBN: 978-1-59643-837-8

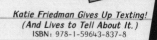

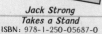

Jack Strong
Takes a Stand
ISBN: 978-1-250-05687-0